CHAPTER ONE

Outside the Community Day Clinic, melting snow had turned to a gray, dirty slush, the only indication that spring was coming to this dismal sector of Chicago's North Side. It wasn't much more colorful inside the austere examining room, Nina Bateman decided. Instead of gray, the interior of the free clinic was a grimy ecru color, walls unadorned by the cheerful paintings that lined corridors of hospitals where patients paid for the services rendered. Taking the thermometer out of a scrawny and frightened youngster's mouth, Nina felt an often recurring hunger for color, for beauty, for something beyond the grimness of her surroundings.

She had walked from the unexciting apartment she shared with her mother this morning. There had been the usual sights and sounds of the old neighborhood—impatient drivers honking as they squished their way through streets still piled with sooty snow at the curbs; two old winos discussing some weighty international problem as they passed the time until Sid opened the doors to his Five-Star Liquor and Deli; the sound of hissing steam from the In-At-Ten-Out-By-Five Laundry and Dry Cleaners. This morning, more than ever, she had missed trees. There ought to be trees, she had thought. Short of walking by way of the park, which had become a mugger's paradise in recent years, there was no possibility of knowing April was approaching because elms and sycamores and maples were leafing. Gray. Everything she looked at, once she had parted from the spindly geraniums and herb plants on the kitchen sill, was uniformly gray.

It was different in the North Shore suburb from which Dr. Mark Danover had driven this morning, Nina realized. What sort of house did he live in? There would be a neatly trimmed rolling lawn, she guessed. It would be studded with pfitzers and meticulously trimmed hedges. There were trees, she was certain—perhaps a cherry tree that would explode in blossoms if the weather continued unseasonably warm. Dr. Danover's background, his life, was as different from Nina's as the scenery that surrounded them.

Until her death, last year, Mark's mother had been a leading socialite, chairman of innumerable charitable and civic and cultural organizations. His father, a retired stockbroker, spent most of his time traveling, occasionally writing short pieces on out-of-the-way places for chic travel magazines. He shared the house in which his doctor-son lived, but was seldom in residence.

Nina had garnered these and other facts from the society pages and from gossip in the

SOCIETY NURSE

Jane Converse

CHIVERS

British Library Cataloguing in Publication Data available

This Large Print edition published by BBC Audiobooks Ltd, Bath, 2009.
Published by arrangement with the Author's Estate.

U.K. Hardcover ISBN 978 1 408 44144 2
U.K. Softcover   ISBN 978 1 408 44145 9

Printed and bound in Great Britain by
CPI Antony Rowe, Chippenham and Eastbourne

nurses' dressing room at the clinic. All of the single nurses were fascinated and curious; Dr. Danover was one of the few doctors who gave his time to the clinic without charge. He had a lucrative practice near his home, but he took Tuesday and Thursday afternoons to attend the impoverished patients who filled the waiting rooms at Community Day. Furthermore, if someone mentioned his kindness or his generosity in doing this volunteer work, Mark Danover became embarrassed and impatient; he was doing something he wanted to do and saw no reason to be praised for doing it.

This was the extent of Nina's knowledge of the doctor. These tidbits of information and her own observations were the basis for an acquaintance, she would often remind herself, not for a full-blown love that consumed her thoughts day and night, that made her breath quicken when Mark Danover's voice was heard from down the corridor, that made all the other days of the week nothing more than waiting periods for the next Tuesday, the next Thursday, when she would see him again.

He was uniformly pleasant to her. But, then, he was uniformly pleasant to everyone; there was no encouragement to be found in his warm smiles, his thoughtful gestures ('I'm going to get some coffee from the machine. Can I bring a cup for you, Nina?'), or even from his complimentary remarks. Usually, the compliments were reserved for Nina's professional services. Once, when he had commented on a new hairdo the day that Nina had arrived with her blonde hair cut in a new shag style with wispy bangs, the mere fact that the doctor had noticed the change and liked it was enough to keep her floating for days afterward.

Still, there was the matter of being realistic. When your background was as poor and as unexciting as the neighborhood in which you lived, you didn't allow yourself to have illusions about the Mark Danovers of this world. You surveyed the man's perfect, distinguished features, his tennis-and-golf-at-the-country-club ruggedness, his summers-on-the-family-yacht tan, and you felt small, undistinctive, and unimportant. People called you 'petite,' but you longed for a slinky, tall model's figure. Boys from the neighborhood, most of whom had grown up to drive trucks or work as clerks at Marshall Field's department store, called you 'pretty,' but you knew that your face was hardly spectacular, your mouth kept from being too large because it was balanced by equally large blue-gray eyes. The dark lashes were an asset. You stared into the mirror at times, not wholly displeased by what you saw, but wishing for . . . for what? Some elusive quality that people defined as 'class.' 'Pretty' was not enough to compensate for your other failings in the eyes of someone like

Mark Danover.

This Thursday afternoon was a case in point. There had been a steady stream of screamers among the children. Mark's soft-spoken voice, his complete ease under any and all circumstances, had made the scene tolerable. When the last patient had left the small examining room in which Nina assisted him, the doctor said calmly, 'Had ourselves a circus today.'

Nina agreed with a nod. 'I don't know how you manage to stay so cool.'

An approving if tired smile was flashed in Nina's direction. 'I didn't see you going into hysterics. Not even when the little Pucci kid almost sank his teeth into your wrist.'

'He's scared to death of shots,' Nina said. 'Poor kid.'

'They're all poor kids,' the doctor said. 'I don't mean just in terms of money or lack of it.' He was slipping out of his white jacket, walking toward the closet door. Nina stripped the disposable covering from the examining table. 'I get cold chills when I talk to some of their mothers. Good intentions, usually, but so abysmally ignorant. Just their lack of insight into kids, their lack of psychological know-how!' Getting into his suit coat, then reaching for the topper he had hung in the closet, Mark Danover shook his head dismally. 'As if the kids weren't scarred enough living in an area like this. I find it depressing just to drive

5

through it. Imagine what it would be like living here? Stuck here all your life?'

Nina had been thinking along the same lines earlier. Now, she felt suddenly defensive. 'You don't have to be scarred because you don't live in a rich neighborhood, Doctor. You . . . might be a little self-conscious about it, when you're around somebody who's been luckier. But it's not a *bad* place. We have some awfully nice people living around us.'

The doctor turned to face her, looking uncomfortable for the first time since Nina had known him. 'We?'

'I live within walking distance of the clinic,' Nina told him. There was almost a touch of pride in her voice. 'I have, since I was twelve. When my father died.'

'Oh, look, I didn't mean to sound like a . . . like a snob.' Mark Danover's dark eyes, always serious, were looking intently into Nina's. 'But I did, didn't I? I was putting down something I don't know the first thing about. I apologize.'

He smiled, and Nina responded with a smile of her own. 'It's all right. Nobody who lives here claims it compares with the Riviera. It's just that not many people live around here by choice. It's a matter of, well, circumstances. Some of the people don't know there's a better way to live. Some of us do, but a nurse's salary, after all the deductions, doesn't go all that far.'

'You live alone?' The doctor was dressed to leave, but he lingered near the doorway.

6

'No. If I were alone, maybe I'd find a couple of other R.N.'s to share an apartment with. In a nicer area.'

'I know you aren't married.'

Self-consciously, Nina glanced at her left hand. He had noticed the absence of a ring; he knew that she was called 'Miss Bateman.' 'You know I'm not. No, I live with my mother.'

Why was he still here, asking personal questions, when the replies couldn't possibly have any meaning for him? 'Your mother's dependent on you?'

Nina shook her head. 'No, she works.'

'Another R.N. ?'

'No. She's a grocery checker. Actually, between us, we could probably afford a better place. But Mom's used to the apartment we live in. She has her friends in the neighborhood. She goes to a place down the street to play bingo, and the manager at the movie theater knows her by name. She wouldn't dream of moving.'

'What about you?'

Nina avoided the questioning stare. 'I might dream. But it's convenient for me. I have a little car, but I don't need it to get to work. I can walk.' She shrugged, almost defiantly. 'It works out very well for me.'

The inquisition was still not over. 'But your mother's not dependent on you for . . . you know . . . meals, any sort of care.'

'She's self-sufficient. It happens that I

7

usually fix dinner because I get home earlier, but my mom could manage on her own very nicely.'

'Except for your company? That must mean a lot to her, if she's widowed . . . alone.'

Nina released a sigh. 'As long as the TV set's working, or there's a good bingo game going on down the block, or a good movie playing, I think I could go to Mombasa on a lion hunt and I wouldn't be missed.' Nina returned the now intense stare. 'Doctor, my mother's one of those women you were talking about a while ago. She lives in a shallow little world all her own. And, as far as being psychologically oriented, forget it. She can't possibly know what my needs are, because I don't think she's ever known me. We're just two people who live in the same apartment and try not to get into each other's way.'

'But that sounds awful!'

'I know of worse situations,' Nina said. 'We don't fight, at least. I like my job. I . . . get out. Dates. Not a wild, exciting social life, but I don't have to spend my evenings with a good book.'

'But you do?'

'A lot of the time.' Nina thrust her chin up in the air. 'I happen to *like* good books.'

'Are you in a big rush to get back to one? I'd like to talk to you for a while, Nina.'

Mark's request caught her unawares. 'I guess . . . I could do that. Why would you, I

8

mean, why would you want to talk to me?'

The doctor laughed. 'A lot of men could point out the obvious reasons. But, at the moment, my reason is purely aboveboard. And professional.'

Nina felt a slight pang of disappointment, yet the prospect of an off-duty conversation with Mark Danover was exciting. Minutes later (after she had experienced the satisfaction of having other nurses enviously watch her leave the building with the doctor), Nina was seated across the table from the man she loved at a restaurant frequented by the clinic staff.

'It leaves a lot to be desired, atmosphere-wise,' Mark commented, looking around the garishly lighted chrome and plastic decor. 'But what it lacks in atmosphere it makes up.'

'In good food?' Nina wrinkled her nose. 'I've had lunch here a few times. You can't fool me.'

Mark laughed again. She was seeing a less sober side of him, and that was reward enough. 'I was trying to think of something it makes up for with, but, so far, nothing's come to mind. It's got to have something going for it.' He gave Nina's hand a friendly pat. 'Good company.'

They laughed together, not once but many times, while they waited for their dinners to be served. Most of their patients were not vehicles for humor, but enough funny things had happened that afternoon to keep the conversation sprightly. It wasn't until their desserts were set before them that Nina realized that this was not purely a social meeting.

'I don't know why it didn't occur to me sooner,' the doctor said. 'I've been wanting a special nurse for this case quite a while. Maybe I never thought of you as being available. And maybe you're not. But, from what you've told me about your home life, it just might be appealing to you.'

'A special assignment? In a hospital?'

'In a private home.'

Nina felt bewildered. 'I've never done special duty work. I've never worked anywhere except the clinic. And I'm satisfied with my job. More than satisfied. I find it . . . you know. The old, trite word that's as badly kicked around as "dedicated."'

' "Fulfilling," ' the doctor guessed.

'Uh-huh. I feel needed. I feel useful. And it's close to home.'

'The job I'm talking about would mean moving into the patient's house.' Mark toyed with his dessert spoon, obviously uninterested in the uninspired-looking custard. He looked out of place in this setting; a second-rate restaurant, chosen for its convenience, was no place for him. 'I may as well tell you about the case before I ask you to consider it. I know that you've had a lot of experience with diabetics at the clinic. I was impressed with

10

your familiarity with control through diet—
your knowledge of metabolism balance, with
the need to adjust insulin doses and types as
the patient's condition varies.'

'I've thought about making it a specialty,'
Nina conceded. 'At one time, I thought about
becoming a dietician.'

'Well, your interest was obvious to me.
That's why I wondered why I hadn't thought of
you for this job sooner.'

'There must be serious complications,' Nina
guessed. 'Most of the diabetics I know manage
without a nurse. I've even showed twelve-year-
old kids how to test for acetone and sugar.
And you know that most of our clinic patients
give themselves their own insulin injections.'

'Yes, I know. This happens to be a . . . a
special case. The young lady I'm concerned
about couldn't possibly be trusted to handle
urine tests and insulin shots. She's . . .' Mark
Danover's face lighted with a knowing half-
smile. 'Let's say that she lives in a dream
world. And that she's a trifle squeamish.'

'But you don't need an R.N. for the job,
unless . . .'

'I wouldn't, if the girl didn't have a
whacked-out mother I don't trust. We could
get a reasonably competent housekeeper to
keep the diet under control and to watch the
blood sugar. But, believe me, there are
extenuating circumstances. Not the least of
which is an emotional factor. You know, I'm

sure, that emotional stress has a bearing on the patient's condition.'

'In any disease.' Nina agreed. 'In diabetes, there's a definite physical reaction.'

'There, you see? You *do* understand. And that's why I'd like your help,' Mark said. 'The girl is almost eighteen.'

'Overweight, I suppose?'

'No. No, she's not in that classic category. Cindy's rather tall, willowy. She's been my patient for three years. And my neighbor for longer than that. My immediate neighbor.'

'Neighbor?' A faintly hopeful thought stirred in Nina's mind. If she accepted the assignment, she would be living next door to the doctor. Inevitably, she would see him often—more often than Tuesday and Thursday afternoons in a busy clinic where there was barely time to take care of the patients let alone time for personal conversations. 'With you living nearby, I wouldn't think . . .'

'I have a heavy schedule,' Mark said. 'I want someone who's right there at all times. No risk of my being out on an emergency call when Cindy needs her insulin. There'll be a tight routine of tests. You know how to do those, but I'd set up a program for you, of course.' He hesitated, as though there was more to tell, something he seemed reluctant to say. 'One of the reasons I'd like you for the job is your age. You'd make a good companion for Cindy, and

12

she needs someone she can confide in. Get close to.'

'You said there was an emotional problem.'

'The girl's mother creates it. Faye's comparatively young, in her early forties. She had big ideas for Cindy. She still has.'

'Career ideas?'

'No. Marrying her off to someone with money. Someone "distinguished," as she puts it.' Mark smiled sheepishly. 'Me.'

'I don't think I'd want to get embroiled in . . .'

'Fortunately, Cindy has more sense than her mother. She's very much in love with a young man I brought into her life. Dave Tolson. He's in med school, poor as a church mouse, too proud to accept help from me or from my father, but Grade-A doctor material. He was doing yard work last summer around my place when he and Cindy met. Faye nearly went through the ceiling. In fact, she's still going through the ceiling.'

'Why?'

'The Calverts are upper crust, Nina. Tops in the social register. And, especially since her husband died and left a bloody fortune, most of it in a trust fund for Cindy, Mrs. Calvert's been determined that her daughter isn't going to—what is the phrase she uses?—Take a step down. She spent a fantastic amount of money getting Cindy ready for a debut that would make history. And Cindy refused to play the

13

game.'

'Refused to "come out"? Isn't that what they call it?'

Mark nodded, looking amused. 'She used her illness. That's something I'd like to see the girl cured of! Using diabetes as a way of getting what she wants. You know that, barring serious complications, there's no reason why a diabetic can't live a perfectly normal life. Providing that the disease is controlled with insulin and diet . . . well, I don't have to explain that to you. But that illness game works two ways. The girl's mother controls Cindy by treating her like an invalid. It's a way to stop her from having dates. Forces the girl to play the same game in order to see Dave.'

Nina made a mock shuddering motion. 'At my house, we've always been too busy raising the rent money to play games with each other.' She sighed, her initial interest in the job fading. 'I don't think I'd be qualified to play referee, Doctor. I don't think I'd have the patience. Two rich, spoiled women . . .'

'Wait until you meet the patient before you write her off,' Mark said. 'She's a wonderful person, Nina. And she needs help. Before she's physically and emotionally destroyed, she needs help. I think you could give it to her.'

'You said she's going on eighteen. It shouldn't be long before she's legally of age to stand up to her mother.'

'I want her strong enough to be able to

14

stand up to a showdown,' Mark said. 'Not just emotionally, although I think moral support from someone who cares about her would be invaluable. *Physically.*'

'With good care, how could there be any doubt about that?'

'"With good care,"' Mark echoed. 'That's the crux of the issue. There's another element I haven't mentioned to you. Faye Calvert's in love. Making an utter fool out of herself over a man fifteen years her junior. She'd like to see Cindy married and out of her hair so that she could do her own thing.'

'Well, that's not too unusual,' Nina commented. 'I'm a little confused. She sounds like a possessive woman, keeping her daughter confined, making an invalid of her. But, on the other hand, you say she wants to . . .'

'To be free of the responsibility. Providing that Cindy marries money and prestige, of course. No, the problem's more complex than that. It's what this man does for a living that concerns me.'

'What's that?'

'Oh, he had a brief, *very* brief, career as an actor. He didn't get too far in Hollywood, but he's learned to apply what talent he has to charming well-heeled widows, like Mrs. Calvert. I'd have no objections. If Faye wants to believe this character is as insanely in love with her as she is with him, that's her business. She can afford to be taken. But Cindy can't.'

'If the girl's money is in a trust fund'—Nina reached for her coffee cup—'I don't know much about these things, but aren't there lawyers or trustees or something to protect a minor in a case like this?'

'He's not going to get Cindy's money.' Mark looked suddenly grim. 'The stakes are higher than that. Perry—the man's name is Ronald Perry—set himself up as the high guru of a phony religion. It's based on mind-over-matter principles, which I don't put down. Mental attitudes have a lot to do with a person's physical well-being. But Perry's added a whole lot of mumbo-jumbo of his own. And he has Faye so completely sold on his ability to cure *anything* that, lately, she's been making noises implying that the whole medical fraternity is composed of charlatans.'

'He's a . . . sort of faith healer?'

'He makes it sound more complicated than that. Very secretive. Very mysterious. Only the privileged disciples can understand his philosophy. Faye Calvert's determined to be number one on the list. And she's so anxious to hang on to this gigolo—that's the only word that comes to mind when I think of him—so anxious to keep him, that she's supporting his whole operation.'

'Even though he doesn't have money? Isn't in the social register?'

'Right. What's sauce for the daughter apparently isn't sauce for mama. For a while

16

there, I thought Faye was on a concentrated campaign to rope my dad. He took off for parts unknown to escape the possibility.' Mark grinned, then after a moment's reflection was serious again. 'That was before Ron Perry swept the lady and her bankbook off their feet.'

They were silent while a waitress refilled their coffee cups. When she had gone, Nina asked, 'Are you worried about this man's influence on—what did you say her name was—Mrs. Calvert?'

'Calvert. Yes.' Mark pondered for a moment. 'I've listened to her rave about the guy and his theories enough to be concerned, yes. Fortunately, Faye's too anxious to sweep me into the family to do anything I'd disapprove of. Trouble is, one of these days I'm going to have to make it finally clear that I think of Cindy as a patient. A nice, unfortunate, overly romantic kid I watched grow up. Not a marriage prospect, God knows. And when I do that, I'm going to be the worst of the quacks in Faye's eyes. She just might start applying her boyfriend's methods.'

'She wouldn't risk her daughter's life . . .'

'With a woman like that—a headstrong, kooky, in-love woman who's afraid of spending the rest of her life alone—you can't know what to think. I've convinced her that Cindy should have full-time nursing care for a while, at least. Her rule about "no dates, no overexertion" wouldn't hold water unless she agreed. I was going to check the nurses' registry tomorrow. And then you and I got to talking and it occurred to me that this could be as good for you as it'd be for my patient.'

By the time they had finished their coffees, Nina had been given a description of the kind of life she would lead, for a few months at least, if she took the job. The pleasant surroundings, a private room, the company of wealthy, interesting people, a charming young patient who thrived on music and poetry and love for an impoverished medical student, all had appeal. There was no need to be concerned about getting back her job at the clinic if the new assignment didn't work out; there would *always* be a place for her at Community Day when she was ready to return. And the thought of getting away from her drab apartment, the dull evenings spent in wordless boredom watching television with her mother, or reading in total silence when her mother found some petty pleasures elsewhere, was as intriguing as Mark Danover had apparently hoped it would be. Certainly the promise of a salary considerably higher than the one she drew at the clinic was a motivating factor.

But, finally, there was one personal point that swayed her, one clinching argument in favor of becoming Cindy Calvert's private nurse. The Calvert home was next door to the house in which Mark lived. Even if it had been barren of trees and beauty for which she yearned, Nina would have made the decision. Living close by, caring for a patient who obviously meant a great deal to the doctor, she would see him daily. Just knowing that Mark wanted her there was a reason, however slim, for hope.

CHAPTER TWO

Nina's impressions of how the well-to-do live had all come from movies and television. Although the Calvert house was not quite as impressive as some structures she had seen in Hollywood films, walking up to the wide double doors of the huge colonial house was an awesome experience. It seemed inconceivable that this enormous red-brick structure, with its row of massive white columns giving it the air of a misplaced plantation house, should be occupied by only two people.

She was not disappointed in the landscape; it was as green and as manicured as she had imagined it would be. As they walked from the wrought-iron-gated driveway to the wide entryway, Mark Danover made a careless gesture indicating a barely visible gray stone edifice just beyond a row of neatly trimmed hedges. 'That's where I live,' he said. If he

19

expected Nina to be impressed, he gave no indication of it. They were here to introduce Mrs. Calvert and her daughter to the new nurse; this was not a social visit.

Minutes after Nina and the doctor had been admitted and led into a drawing room furnished with ornate French antiques, a delicately hued rug that Mark dismissed carelessly as 'a reasonably good Aubusson,' and several ornately framed oil paintings that had probably cost more than the average R.N. earns in five years, the prim, unsmiling maid returned to announce that Mrs. Calvert would be with them shortly.

'Shortly' turned out to be a period of ten minutes. And when Faye Calvert made her appearance, it was easy to understand why it had taken her so long. She had undoubtedly prepared for her entrance the way a movie star prepares to go on stage before her peers at an Academy Awards presentation. She swept into the room wearing a bright hand-printed caftan, her neck weighted down with a mass of exotic chains and pendants, also of foreign origin, also obviously hand-crafted. Like all women who cannot gracefully acknowledge their age, she flashed an unnatural youthfulness, made possible by an intricate, high-piled coiffure, dark eyelashes that were too long and too upswept to belong to their present owner, and coral lipstick that somehow managed to accentuate rather than

20

conceal the thinness of her mouth. Her hair glistened golden blonde under the light of the crystal chandelier. Her fingers all but sagged under a collection of unique one-of-a-kind opal and other gemstone rings. Yet, in spite of the dazzling picture she had so painstakingly prepared, Faye Calvert struck Nina as someone she would rather not know.

She smiled her welcome, of course, as Nina was introduced. But there was something cold and calculating about the smile, matching the insincere expression in her heavy-lidded hazel eyes. Nina's first reaction was, She doesn't like me. On closer observation, she added a footnote: She doesn't like many people. I'm probably in good company.

It appeared, however, that Mark Danover was one of the chosen few who had Mrs. Calvert's approval. When they were seated, and the woman's offer of cocktails had been politely declined, Faye Calvert said, 'I'll swear, darling, this regimen you've imposed on Cindy gets more confusing every day. How can you have her on fifty-two units one day and forty-two the next? You know I'm too squeamish to plunge a needle into my own child, and Cindy can't bring herself to do it. And I get confused, trying to tell our housekeeper what's needed when you keep changing the dosage.'

'That's precisely why you need a nurse here,' Mark said evenly. 'I think Miss Bateman can explain why the dosage isn't consistent.'

21

Nina felt like a child who has been called upon to recite for the household guests. 'It's a matter of control, Mrs. Calvert. When the amount of physical activity changes, and the amount of food taken in changes, the insulin requirement is going to change accordingly. If your daughter's more active than usual, the insulin need is going to be changed. We have to keep testing the amount of blood sugar . . .'

Nina's explanation was dismissed with a wave of Mrs. Calvert's hands. 'I'll never understand it. I suppose Mark is right. Cindy needs a professional to look after her.' She surveyed Nina as though she were examining a somewhat questionable pot roast. 'I suppose if Miss Bateman is going to live in, I should have Cindy meet her.'

If the interview had ended at that moment, Nina would have erased the new venture from her mind then returned to Community Day Clinic the next morning with the full intention of remaining on the job as long as she was wanted. It was meeting Cindy Calvert that changed her mind.

Faye Calvert's daughter came into the room bringing a strangely touching beauty with her. She was as far removed from Nina's preconceived image of a spoiled, overly rich brat as it was possible to imagine. Tall, graceful, moving as though she were propelled by poetry, Cindy was as natural as her mother was artificial. Her long dark hair was parted at

22

the center and allowed to fall carelessly over her thin shoulders. She was pale, but the paleness gave a classic Grecian appearance to her finely chiseled features. Nina thought of her posing for Renaissance painters, inspiring artists with visions of perfect Madonnas, smiling wistfully, gentle as April rain.

Cindy's eyes were amazingly lustrous, yet there was a quality about her that made Nina think that she needed someone to care for her. And the warmth that radiated between prospective nurse and prospective patient was immediate and palpable.

'What do you think, dear?' Mrs. Calvert asked in her cool, imperious tone. 'Don't jump to conclusions. Remember that you and Miss Bateman will be spending a great deal of time together.'

Nina flushed under the calloused tone that reduced her to a serving maid. Cindy smiled at her shyly and said, 'I think it would be wonderful.'

'Well, what our doctor says to do is what we do,' Mrs. Calvert said. She made it clear that hiring the nurse was not her idea. She also shot Mark a fond look that told him she would approve of anything he thought best for her child. 'I know how important Cindy's well-being is to you, darling,' she said to the doctor. To Nina, as if it were necessary to make matters clear, she said, 'Dr. Danover and my daughter have been very close for years and years. I'm sure he's told you, Miss Bateman, how much they mean to each other.'

Cindy's colorless face took on a pinkish glow. 'Oh, mother . . .' She lowered her gaze to the expensive blue rug at her feet.

Mark let the remark pass over his shoulders. 'We can get to the details, then,' he said in a matter-of-fact tone. 'Maybe Cindy would like to show Miss Bateman . . .'

'Her room. Of course.' Faye Calvert rose to her feet. 'Are you up to it, dear? I can have Leah or Constance . . .'

'Sure, I'm up to it,' Cindy said. She had walked over to Nina, who had risen to her feet. Linking her arm through Nina's, she said, 'C'mon see what you think. You'll go stir crazy, probably, the way I do, but you won't have to do anything heavy or messy. We have a housekeeper and one live-in maid. I guess you'll just have to give me those stupid shots and do all those dumb tests. The rest of the time, maybe we can rap.'

Nina was pleased with the girl's carefree attitude, with her tinkling laughter. She left the room with her new patient, aware of Faye Calvert's cold eyes following her, still wondering if working at the clinic wasn't a better idea.

They had examined a smartly furnished room, with adjoining bath, that had been set aside for guests and now was intended as quarters for Cindy's nurse. 'It's just across the

24

hall from where I hang out,' Cindy said brightly. 'Wanna see my room? It's a mess, but you know how it is. I don't like the maid coming in. I like to be by myself.'

The girl smiled, looking at Nina as though she were positive her new friend would understand. 'When I'm not with the right people, I mean.'

Nina was ushered into a spacious bedroom boasting a canopied bed, matching chintz ruffled draperies at a window that overlooked the hedge-bordered driveway and the front lawn. There was a view of the curving street with its rows of Lombardy poplars, new leaves budding with the promise of spring. There were no pictures of movie stars or pop artists on the walls. Instead, Cindy had decorated her room with simply framed etchings of her favorite poets—Byron, Shelley, and Keats. A stereo set, left on during Cindy's absence, filled the room with a Mozart string quartet. Nina had the sensation of walking into the past, although the girl who occupied the room was fresh and bright in spite of her illness.

'I hope you like poetry,' she heard Cindy saying. 'And classical music. Until I met Dave I had no one to share them with. You'll have to meet Dave. He's a very special friend of mine.'

'I've heard about him,' Nina said.

Cindy's eyes widened. 'You *have?*' Then, after a moment's reflection: 'Mark told you about him. Mark thinks he's great. And he is, too. He's going to be a doctor. I mean, a real doctor-doctor who doesn't care about getting rich, like some do. Not that I'm putting Mark down. He does volunteer work at some real poor clinic, and everything. I guess you know about it, if you work there. *Used* to work there.' Cindy gave Nina a sudden, quick hug. 'Oh, wow, it's so great that you're going to be here. Somebody to *talk* to.' Released from the impulsive, almost embarrassing embrace, Nina caught a glimpse of the girl's terrible loneliness. 'Maybe I'll bore you. I mean, I love poetry. My mother thinks I'm out of my gourd. But Dave . . . Dave Tolson . . . he and I, when we can get together, we read it back and forth, and he's taught me so much. He's . . . oh, wow, Miss Bateman, he's done so much for me!'

'Nina.'

'Huh?'

'If I'm going to work here, I'd like you to call me Nina.'

It seemed that the dark eyes misted over, but Cindy was too changeable to let a sentimental mood pervade. In the next second she was showing her new nurse a portfolio of poetry she had written herself, disparaging it, smiling, 'It's pretty corny, but you know how it is. I get to thinking about Dave and all this flowery stuff comes out. You don't have to read any of this if you don't want to. *He* likes it, but that's because . . . that's only because . . .'

26

'He loves you,' Nina guessed.

There was a long, tense silence, during which Nina was sorry she had made the obvious remark. Then, Cindy half-whispered, 'That's okay, isn't it? Mark keeps telling me I'll be able to live a . . . you know . . . a normal life. Get married and even have children. Is that true? Maybe he's just being kind. Dave's studied up on diabetes and *he* says it's true, but maybe they're just being nice to me. If I'm going to get well, why don't I get to go out and do whatever I want to do? Go out with Dave, go to dances and concerts? I don't *feel* sick. Tired, a lot of the time. But if I thought, if I was *sure,* that I'll get cured some day . . .'

'Diabetics don't get "cured,"' Nina told her. 'If we're going to spend a lot of time together, we're going to start out by being honest with each other, Cindy. So far, there's no real cure for your problem. But it's not exactly a disease, either. It's an imbalance in the system. With the right diet, with carefully controlled injections of insulin, the situation is kept under control. It's that simple.'

'I *could* go out with Dave then, couldn't I?'

Cindy's question was so heavy with melancholy that Nina hesitated to give her an answer. She hadn't started on the job yet, and she was already in a position where Mrs. Calvert had to be contradicted. Still, with those sad young eyes imploring her for the right response, Nina could not do otherwise

27

than to tell her the truth. 'If you watch your diet, if we check your blood sugar regularly and manage the insulin accordingly, you can do anything any of your friends can do, Cindy. And that includes dating. Going to parties. Whatever.'

'That's what the doc keeps telling my mom.' Suddenly, erratically, the girl picked up a stuffed plush kitten from her bed and slammed it against the wall. 'She'd let me go out with *him*,' Cindy cried. 'With Mark. He's like an older brother. I'm just a kid to him, for Pete's sake. But I keep getting this business about how we grew up together. Grew up together! He's almost old enough to be my father. He's in his *thirties!*' The way Cindy said it, 'thirties' meant being ready for an old people's home. 'Anyway, Mark only likes me because he feels sorry for me. And he likes Dave, too.' Mention of the young man's name had shifted Cindy into a mellower mood almost instantly. 'Just about everybody loves Dave. You will, too.' She released a long sigh. 'Just about everybody but my mother. And what's he ever done to make her hate him the way she does? Miss Bateman . . . Nina, he's just about the most beautiful, the most wonderful person in the whole world!'

Nina felt herself on shaky ground. She was being hired, after all, by the girl's mother. A nurse didn't make disparaging personal remarks about the person who employed her.

28

'Maybe she just feels very protective, Cindy. You can't really blame her. She cares about you and—'

'And she thinks I ought to marry the doctor next door,' Cindy said. The bitter tone was erased in the next sentence; it was apparently part of Cindy's personality to switch from one mood to another within a few seconds. 'I know she loves me. She's been awfully good to me. If it wasn't for me, my mom could be leading a life of her own. She's still pretty young, as mothers go, if you know what I mean. And she has this awfully close friend. Sometimes I think I'm standing in her way.' There was another awkward and thoughtful silence, and then Cindy was laughing. 'I'm being such a cornball, you'll change your mind about moving in here. Look, everything's fine. I'll work it out. But, it's going to be so neat to have somebody to talk to. You can't begin to imagine, Miss . . .'

'Nina.'

'Nina. You can't know what it's been like.'

Nina had a better concept of what it had been like moments later when she and Cindy returned to the room with the Aubusson rug.

Mark and Mrs. Calvert had been joined by a new visitor, though from his familiarity with the place it was clear that Ronald Perry considered himself more than a guest. Introductions were made, and Nina found herself being stared at by a foppish and almost too theatrically handsome young man, who made it a point to brush hands with Faye Calvert more than was necessary.

Ron Perry could not have been older than Mark, which placed him somewhere in his thirties. He was dressed in a mod beige suit and paisley shirt. Two rings on his professionally manicured hands almost duplicated those that Faye Calvert was wearing. His hair, modishly long and expertly styled, was a wavy, light brown. Greenish-blue eyes, half bored, half on the lookout for opportunities that must not be missed, gave a 'not bad' sweep of approval as he acknowledged Nina's existence. 'I was just telling Dr. Danover that one of these days soon, his profession will be obsolete. I expect that must apply to your line of work, too, Miss Bateman.'

Mark was looking at the man as though he were a bug that had crawled into the room, and since stomping him would ruin the Aubusson rug, was to be ignored. Mrs. Calvert's expression was one of worship mingled with an inviting sexy gaze. Cindy seemed to have retired to a private world of her own. She studied her fingertips and appeared removed from the conversation.

Nina decided to accept the challenge. 'Oh, I think M.D.'s and R.N.'s are going to be around for a while,' she said. 'We still seem to be needed.'

Ron Perry fixed her with a cool stare. His

voice took on the quality of a mystic pronouncing some esoteric wisdom. 'Physical attention will be needed only as long as humanity remains unenlightened,' he droned. 'Once the wisdom of the ancient masters becomes common knowledge, bodily ills will be disposed of by the enlightened mind as the insubstantial matters they are.'

'Fine,' Nina said. 'In the meantime, though, you don't mind if they keep the surgical wards at County open. A ruptured appendix can be such a nuisance to someone who doesn't know all you do.'

Faye Calvert threw her a poisonous look. Mark laughed out loud. Cindy smiled her appreciation, then, catching a disdainful glance from her mother, went back to staring at her nails.

Ron Perry, who had been introduced as the *Reverend* Mr. Perry, assumed a lofty pose, as though he could not lower himself to arguing with someone so abysmally uninformed. It was strange, Nina thought; usually she liked almost everyone she met. Here, within half an hour, she had made the acquaintance of two eminently detestable people.

It was only her immediate rapport with Cindy Calvert, and Mark's desire to have her on the job, that kept Nina from bowing out of the situation. There was a brief discussion of hours, moving arrangements, and salary. Ron Perry said nothing during these negotiations, letting everyone know that he was above such mundane matters.

'Do you drive?' Mrs. Calvert asked when the money matter had been settled. 'There may be times when you'll be called upon to get Cindy to the hospital or to Dr. Danover's office. And you might want to go home occasionally. There isn't any public transportation to speak of.'

'I drive,' Nina told her, 'I have my own car.'

Mrs. Calvert had gotten to her feet, indicating that the interview had ended. 'Then we can expect you next Friday. Can you find your way out of here? Until people get accustomed to all these curving streets . . .'

'I brought Nina out,' Mark said, getting up and walking to her side. 'I'm driving her home.'

Faye Calvert's face tensed. It was clear that she had expected the doctor to linger on. 'Oh. Of course.' She forced herself into a false smile as Mark exchanged a few words with her daughter, turning to Nina and saying pointedly, 'Dr. Danover's been such a dear friend to Cindy. They've known each other for . . .'

'Years and years,' Nina said, repeating the earlier warning Mrs. Calvert had issued. 'I know. He's very fond of your daughter.'

Amazingly, Ron Perry laughed. It was a vindictive, under-his-breath sort of laugh, but he seemed pleased that someone had seen through Mrs. Calvert's lack of subtlety.

Mark and Nina were at the door when the chimes sounded. Without waiting for the maid, Mark opened the door. They found themselves face to face with a tall, thin, freckled, auburn-haired young man, probably just barely in his twenties. He looked shocked. 'Doc! Hey, what a trip! I just stopped at your house and the lady who works for you said you were probably over here. I saw your car in the driveway.'

'You drove all the way out here just to see me?' Mark grinned. 'Nina, this is David Tolson. Dave, this is Nina Bateman. She's going to be Cindy's nurse.'

The introductions were acknowledged in the open doorway.

Dave Tolson's smile was as open as his face. 'Cindy's nurse? Man, that's good news. When do you start, Miss Bateman?'

'Next Friday. I have to give notice at the clinic. Get my personal belongings together,' Nina told the young man.

He shook his head back and forth, looking relieved. 'Great. They need *somebody* in this house.' He was peering past them. 'Cindy still up? I've got a few hours. Rammed through a paper I had to write. I guess you remember how it was, Doc.'

'I remember,' Mark said.

'Yeah. Well, I have some more studying to do tonight, but I had some gas in the old jalopy, and I thought why not come out and see Cindy.' The already pinkish face flushed a deeper shade. 'And you, too, of course. I've been wanting to get together with you.'

Mark accepted the social lie, giving Dave a friendly punch to the shoulder. 'Sure you have.' He glanced backward. 'Is she expecting you? Cindy didn't say . . .'

'No. I tried calling earlier, but Mrs. Calvert said'—Dave scowled—'never mind,' he said quietly. 'I got the impression Cindy was asleep and didn't want to see me.'

'Wrong impression,' Mark said softly. '*Two* wrong impressions. She's wide awake. I don't have to tell you she'll be . . .'

'Mother, I don't want to go to bed! I'm not tired! If that's Dave at the door—'

Cindy's voice, rising to a high, sibilant pitch, froze them in position.

'I should really have seen Mark and that nurse to the door.' That was Faye Calvert's voice, trembling with nervousness. There was a brittle laugh. 'Though Mark's been our neighbor for so many years, he just runs in and out. Excuse me, darling. And Cindy dear, I really do think you should go to your room. There's no point in our hiring a nurse for you if you aren't going to cooperate.'

'I thought I heard Dave—'

'Some day, I'm going to forget she's Cindy's mother and I'm gonna strangle that witch.' Dave Tolson's boyish face had taken on a

34

furious cast. He had muttered the words facetiously, but there was no mistaking the intensity of his feeling.

Mark repeated the shoulder punch. 'Hang on, fella.' He turned to Nina. 'Excuse the delay . . . little bit of business to take care of.'

If Nina had not known before that moment that she loved Mark, she was left with no doubts when he turned around, walked back into the house, through the long hallway that led to the drawing room. He had linked one arm through Nina's and another through that of the startled medical student, virtually pulling them along with him in his return to the room in which Faye Calvert, her 'spiritual adviser,' and Cindy stood facing one another like sparring prize fighters.

'Look who dropped by!' Mark said cheerfully.

Nina had a fleeting glimpse of Mrs. Calvert's poisonous expression, of the pure joy radiating from Cindy's face, the blasé amusement of Ronald Perry. The young people hurried toward each other as if they had been pulled by magnets.

Mark was aware of the consternation he had caused, but he seemed to be deriving pleasure from it. 'We met Dave at the door,' he said blithely. 'Nice break. You said you and the "reverend" had a meeting at his "truth center" later tonight. That would have left Cindy with nobody to talk with. Nice break, no? I'm sure the kids have a lot to talk about.'

Mark was looking Faye Calvert in the eye with a no-nonsense expression. Short of infuriating him, there was nothing the woman could do but fake a pleased simper and say, 'Yes. Yes, it's just lovely. Although I don't want Cindy to exert herself.'

Perhaps Ron Perry had fancied a career as an actor, but Faye Calvert's histrionic talents left much to be desired. She was annoyed and angry. But Mark had made it impossible for her to ask Dave Tolson to leave. To make certain that his intentions were clearly understood, the doctor added, 'Cindy isn't a bed case, Faye. As I've been trying to tell you, if we watch her glucose tests and manage the insulin, there's nothing she can't do that any normal teen-aged kid does. In fact, the happier she is and the less emotional turmoil she's subjected to, the better off she's going to be. And that is what we all want, isn't it?'

Mrs. Calvert pretended nonchalance. 'Of course. You couldn't possibly think otherwise, Mark.'

'It's sometimes a matter of *mind* over matter.' Mark had evidently been unable to resist the sarcastic quip. He nodded graciously at Ron Perry.

'Reverend' Ron's nostrils were distended, accenting his supercilious expression. 'You're beginning to understand,' he said.

Nina would not have suspected that Mark

36

was capable of snide mischief. At the clinic he had always appeared serious, if not grave. Now, his dark eyes were bright with the pleasure of accomplishing something that half the company had wanted badly and the other half had not wanted at all. 'You run along to your meeting, Faye, and don't worry about a thing. As Cindy's doctor, I *prescribe* a long conversation with my favorite medical student.' He waved a cheery 'see you later' to the younger people, who were adoring him with their eyes, devastated Faye Calvert with a playful wink, and guided Nina back to the door.

As they drove to Nina's less glamorous neighborhood, Mark talked at length about Dave Tolson. 'This kid's incredible. He worked all the way through high school. And paid his own way through pre-med. Mowing my lawn, among other things. With all the study that's involved, I can't even begin to imagine how he did it. Not only did it, but got straight A's. And he's still pulling straight A's. People like that leave me feeling absolutely second-rate.'

'It can be done,' Nina said. A damp wind was blowing in from Lake Michigan. Earlier, she had left the car window on her side open, enjoying the promise of spring in the air. Now she rolled the window up. 'When you don't have any choice, you'd be amazed at what can be done.'

'Are you talking from experience?' Mark asked.

'Oh, I'm not patting myself on the back. Nursing school isn't any sleigh ride, but it doesn't compare with what Dave's tackled.'

'But you worked your way through? Actually *worked* your way through?'

'It's no big thing,' Nina said. 'It's rough, but it's hardly a miracle.'

'It sounds like a miracle to me. I know how exhausted I used to get, cramming. If I'd had to live on what I made as an intern . . .' Mark shook his head, his eyes never leaving the heavily trafficked throughway.

'My mother couldn't have paid my way through,' Nina told him. 'Even if she could have scraped up the money, she wouldn't have seen the reason for it. She thought I should stay where I was. Expand my part-time job to a full-time career.'

'Doing what?'

Nina managed a laugh, remembering. 'Anytime you want to see potatoes French-fried in volume, call me up. I know more about starch and fat than any dietician in the business.'

'You worked in a—'

'In a greasy spoon. Fast take-out place. If I'd stayed long enough, I'd have gotten promoted to a waitress job, but I managed to graduate before that happened.'

Was Mark patronizing her, reminding her of

the differences in their backgrounds? It didn't seem that he was. If anything, he seemed to be in awe of Nina's accomplishment. He spoke the same way about Dave Tolson. 'The kid almost makes me feel ashamed of myself. I've had it so easy, Nina. So damned easy. I'd watch Dave raking the leaves around my house and think, what a waste of time and talent and energy. I'd still like to help the guy. But he's got some kind of pride thing. I don't want to insult him. Maybe I'd be taking something away from him if I didn't let him do it his way.'

'I think I can understand that,' Nina said. 'No matter how rough it gets, you always have that proud feeling; look, I did this myself. Nobody had to help me. I did it on my own.'

They were still talking about Dave Tolson when Nina directed Mark to the curb in front of her apartment house. She had been somewhat ashamed, earlier, thinking of the impression Mark would get from the shoddy building, the less than desirable neighborhood. Since their conversation about the penniless medical student, she had felt a surge of pride. Astoundingly, Mark sounded almost envious of Dave, envious of *her!*

Mark switched off the motor. 'Let me see you to the door,' he said. But he didn't move to get out of his car.

There was a brief period of quiet, heavy with the rapport that existed between them. Then Nina said something that she had been wanting to say all through the ride home. 'You know what? I don't think I've ever liked anyone as much as I liked you tonight. When you made sure that kid was going to be let inside the Calverts' house.'

Mark looked pleased. In the dim light from the street lamps, his face glowed with pleasure. 'Do *you* know what? I kind of liked myself. Faye wouldn't have let the kid in, otherwise, you know. I figured it was the least I could do. Not just for Dave. For Cindy, too. Those kids are so right for each other. Why can't she see that?'

'Wrong side of the tracks,' Nina said. 'You told me why yourself.'

'Can you picture anything more stupid?' Mark laughed shortly. 'Fortunately, as long as Faye has even the slightest hope of converting me to a son-in-law, she can't get into a hassle with me. I got a tremendous kick out of the whole scene. I'm glad you appreciated it.'

'She really thinks she can get you interested in Cindy?'

'She's convinced that she can. I've told her in so many words that the idea is ridiculous. I've introduced her to girlfriends, just to bring my point home.'

Nina felt alienated, suddenly, at the idea of girlfriends. She could visualize them—smart young women who played tennis with Mark at his country club. Junior League clubs who belonged in Mark's social circle. She was suddenly ashamed of the apartment to which she could not invite Mark because her mother would probably be watching a movie on television, dressed in her sleazy rayon robe, hair up in pink plastic curlers in anticipation of the next day behind the supermarket checking counter. She felt inadequate, even cheap, in the bargain-basement suit she had chosen to wear for her meeting with the Calverts. A moment ago she had felt a surge of pride, but she realized now that Mark had been praising people from another world, the way she herself might congratulate a poor wino who came to the clinic, lauding him because he had done the sensible thing for a change. She wanted to hurry out of the sleek car, run up the stairs to her apartment, and cry.

'I wish I hadn't just arranged a job for you,' she heard Mark saying.

He meant 'a plush job,' but he was too polite to say it.

'I don't want this to seem like I'm expecting to be rewarded. Or have you respond out of . . . well, "gratitude" is too strong a word. Out of appreciation. I'd like this to be because'—Mark's right arm had fallen over her shoulders—'because of what you said a little while ago. That you like me. Because, you know something, Nina? I more than like you. I more than like you a great deal.'

It was easy and natural. His arms closed around her. If the kiss was more brotherly than

41

Nina had hoped it would be, it was so unexpected, so longed for, that the thrill of Mark's lips pressed against hers left Nina breathless.

He didn't say any more than good night after that. There were no promises that this was the beginning of something beyond friendship; it was one of those things that happen casually and irresistibly because the time and the circumstances are right. When he left her at the building door, Mark waved, said he would enjoy having her as a neighbor, and left. He could not have known, Nina was certain, that she would spend a sleepless night reliving a moment that had probably meant so little to him.

CHAPTER THREE

Friday morning Nina moved her personal possessions into the Calvert home, occupying a room that adjoined that of her new patient.

Mrs. Calvert paid little attention to her; it was as though a new maid had been added to the household staff. Busy with her involvement with Ronald Perry, Cindy's mother spent most of her time away from home, and the balance of it getting dressed for the next meeting with her paramour. Except for the housekeeper— a gaunt, wiry, thin-lipped woman named

Constance Bell—Cindy had few human contacts beyond her nurse. And involving the fortyish, prematurely gray housekeeper in a conversation was just short of impossible. She supervised, with grim efficiency, the chores of a plump, rather glassy-eyed maid named Leah, an all-around gardener and handyman who was referred to as 'Pike,' and prepared meals. When her duties were finished, Mrs. Bell retired to her room in the servants' quarters to watch television or, as Cindy put it, 'to write long letters that never get answered.'

With only telephone calls and one of the rarely permitted visits from Dave Tolson to look forward to, Cindy Calvert welcomed companionship the way a drowning man grasps at a life preserver. Their first morning together, after Mark Danover had gone over the diet and insulin regimen that was to be followed and had left for his office, Cindy dropped to a corner of her bed, inviting Nina to sit down in a nearby lounge chair. 'Don't go, please. Let's talk.'

Nina returned the warm smile. 'Sure. I'm going to feel guilty, though. Getting paid for sitting around and talking.'

Cindy closed her eyes for a moment. 'That's . . . oh, you don't know. That's the most important thing you could possibly do for me, Nina.' Her pale features colored slightly, as if in embarrassment. 'I'm not putting down what you're going to do for me, you know,

43

medically. I know that's important if I'm ever going to get well. But you don't know how lonely it gets around here. Sometimes I . . . you know what?' A faint smile crossed Cindy's face. 'I actually talk to myself. Out loud. They're going to come for me with a butterfly net one of these days.'

The girl was forcing the smile. It seemed to Nina that her eyes had misted over. 'You have friends, though, don't you? You've lived in the area for years. I know your mother planned a big coming-out party for you. There must be—'

'There used to be kids my own age,' Cindy said. She was staring out into the garden, almost as though she were still talking to herself. 'There were girls I knew at school. But after I got sick, little by little they stopped coming over. They're in college, most of them. When they're in town, they have dates and they, well, they have better things to do than sit around here feeling sorry for me. I haven't even been out to the club in ages. The country club. I used to play tennis with the kids there. And there'd be dances, usually on Saturday night.'

'Why haven't you gone?' Nina asked.

Cindy turned to her, frowning. 'Because I've been sick. I can't do all those things.' She looked critical, as though an R.N. should have known better than to ask the question.

'Has Dr. Danover told you you can't ever go

out and enjoy yourself?'

Cindy flushed under Nina's direct stare. 'Well, he . . . he tells me I can, if I watch it. But, then, there's all that business of having to take in a lot more calories if I use up too much energy. Nobody's had time to figure all that out.'

'I'm here to figure all that out,' Nina told her. 'Cindy, there isn't a reason in the world why you have to stay cooped up here like an invalid. I'm not going to have anything to do except to see that you stay in balance. I've taken care of lots of diabetic patients. They don't get "cured," understand. But once they know what has to be done to stay fit, they live perfectly normal lives. I think it's insane for you to live here like a recluse when you don't have to.'

Cindy was staring out the window again. 'Maybe you can get that across to my mother.' She sighed, obviously uncomfortable with the subject. 'But if Mark can't make her see it, I doubt that you will. She really worries about me. I don't want to upset her, Nina. She's made so many sacrifices for me . . . done so much.'

Nina came close to asking what the sacrifices were, but she hadn't been hired to cause dissension in the family. She merely nodded, thinking of her own mother's indifference to her moving out of the apartment. There had been an opportunity for

45

'sacrifice' in her own home; she thought of the time she was desperate for money, just before she started out as a probationer. New uniforms and a stopwatch were essential. Her mother had invested in a new television set. But if Mrs. Calvert had gone without something to make Cindy's life more pleasant, what it had been had to be a family secret. Cindy's blind loyalty should not be shaken, however. Nina remained silent, waiting for her attractive young patient to go on.

'The only thing that really bothers me,' Cindy said after a long silence, 'is this business with Mark. Oh, and with Dave, too. With her not liking Dave. I guess Mother's being protective. She figures Dave's got to have some kind of ulterior motive. I guess . . . when I'm twenty-one, I'm going to have a lot of money. She thinks anybody who isn't well-off is going to dope out some way to get at it. And that's not true. She means well, but with Dave . . . it's just not *so*.'

'You're a very pretty girl. You and Dave seem to have a lot in common. And I think Mark . . . Dr. Danover's a pretty good judge of character. *He* seems to encourage your friendship with Dave.'

Cindy's face took on a poetic, dreamy look. 'I know. Mark's been so good to me. And he *does* know what makes people tick. Like, if he didn't, he'd think I was out to . . .' The faraway look disappeared in another cloud of confusion. 'What I mean is, he knows I don't see him the way my mother does. She really thinks we . . . she's always thought someday Mark and I—' Cindy got up from the edge of her bed. 'It's so strange, I can't even talk about it. And sometimes I get so embarrassed. Like, she just keeps pushing us together.'

It was another subject that Nina decided to leave alone. Talking was good therapy for Cindy. She waited, letting the girl express herself when she was ready to.

'Well, anybody with any sense ought to know that Mark's too old for me. He looks at me like a . . . like a *kid*. Anyway, there's no feeling between us, except that I appreciate all he tries to do for me. Making it impossible for Mother to stop Dave from coming over, for one thing. Mark's a friend. One of the only few I've got.'

'But you're not in love with him.' Nina thought that the statement was obvious enough to be safe.

'*Love* with him?' Cindy released a short laugh. 'He's like my father. It's so weird. On one hand, Mother wants to make a big impression on him. But she gets outside advice from you-know-who, and she follows *that* a lot of the time. Sometimes I don't know what's going on. All I know is, Mark would be'—she turned a shy smile toward Nina—'he'd be so neat for *you*. Not that you're old, or anything. I don't mean that. I mean, you're more—'

47

'You mean I'm not in my teens,' Nina said.

'No offense. I thought, the minute you walked into the house with him—I was peeking from my window when he brought you over the first time—I thought, oh, wow, I'll bet he's crazy about her. You looked so pretty and so . . . so sort of scared, like you didn't know what you were getting into, and I knew he'd knock himself out making you feel comfortable.' There was another embarrassed laugh from Cindy. 'Tell me to shut up if I'm talking about something you don't want to talk about. Mother says I'm too romantic. I read so much poetry and I . . . maybe I was born too late, I don't know. The only person I've ever talked to about the way I feel is Dave. He likes Keats and Shelley and Lord Byron, the way I do. It was one of the first things we found out about each other—the things we share. And it's so great, Nina. I don't really need a lot of friends now that I have Dave. He's the most beautiful person I've ever known in my life. I just wish—'

Cindy left the wistful thought hanging in mid-air, but it was easy to discern her meaning. She wished that her mother would understand that she was in love, that someone else loved her, that she needed and wanted love as perhaps no other girl her age could have needed it.

'If Mother would just get to *know* Dave, I'm sure she'd like him. He's so into what he's

48

doing, wanting to get to be a great doctor and to help people. And with all he has to do, working his way through school and having to study as hard as he does, he still finds time for me. I don't want to bore you, your first day here, but one of these days I'll show you some of the poetry he's written to me. Just beautiful thoughts.' Cindy had dropped to the edge of her bed once more. There was so much that she wanted to say, so much that had remained unexpressed because there hadn't been anyone around to listen. Yet she was fearful that her personal longings, her romantic young surge of love, would be tiresome to a new friend. 'I shouldn't bore you with all this. You're probably sorry you ever came here, having to listen to me.'

'Cindy, where did you get the idea that you aren't an interesting person and that people wouldn't want to have your company?' Nina had meant the question as a form of encouragement for a very insecure youngster. She realized almost instantly that she had opened up a subject that was better left to a qualified psychologist.

Cindy's eyes filled with tears. 'How can I be interesting? I'm a drag to everybody—my mother, my doctor, Dave. I don't do anything but listen to Mozart and write corny verses. I can't even take care of myself; I have to have somebody like you to look after me. Sooner or later, Dave's going to get tired of being treated

49

like he had leprosy, and he's going to quit coming over here. There've got to be lots of girls at the university who'd do anything to get his attention. Mark's going to get sick to death of having me shoved at him. And Mother . . .' Cindy made a vague shrugging motion. 'She could be enjoying herself so much more if she didn't have me to worry about. 'Cause, no matter what you say, Nina, she's right. I don't have a lot of energy. I have to watch what I eat and get shots and have a nurse to look after me. Even you, you'll get tired of listening to me. Sometimes I just wish—'

Cindy's wish was left unsaid, but Nina imagined what it might be. Attractive, unspoiled in spite of her affluent upbringing, acutely sensitive, Cindy Calvert had gotten the idea that she wasn't much. Nina thought of Faye Calvert and remembered Dave Tolson's facetious threat: *'Some day I'm going to forget that she's Cindy's mother and I'm gonna strangle that witch!'*

Yet, with all of Mrs. Calvert's bewildering maneuvers to 'protect' her daughter from a poor 'nobody' like Dave, with all her unsubtle and humiliating efforts to promote a marriage between two uninterested parties, and with her incomprehensible demand that Cindy be thought of as a helpless, chronic invalid, Mrs. Calvert was not resented by her only child. It was puzzling. In many ways, Cindy appeared to be hypersensitive, sharply aware

50

of all that was going on around her. Yet she seemed to harbor no malice toward her mother; in fact, as the day progressed, Nina heard her say more than once that she was 'grateful' for her mother's devotion to her. Apparently Cindy had been dictated to for so many years, made to feel so dependent on her mother, that it didn't occur to her that she was being badly mistreated.

One of these days, Nina thought, I'll get Cindy to stand up and fight for her rights. It was too early in the game to do that, however. Nina spent the rest of the day explaining to Cindy how her physical problem was going to be controlled. Cindy had little interest in the management of insulin injections, in body metabolism, in the fact that diabetes was something a victim lived with for a lifetime, although there was no longer any need to think of oneself as helpless or incapacitated. 'That's why you're here, I guess,' the girl said while Nina was trying to acquaint her with a few simple medical facts. 'I trust you. You and Mark. As long as you're here, I don't have to know all these things or worry about them.'

She lived in a dream world, Nina concluded. A dream world in which beautiful music and lovely words removed her from the harsh reality of being a poor-little-rich-girl dominated by a high-strung, neurotic mother. Cindy didn't *want* to know any more than the facts that she was lonely, she was in love, she was a burden to her mother, she should be grateful that people cared about her at all. It had taken years of conditioning to make the girl accept this self-effacing state; the results would not be undone in a few short conversations with a newly engaged R.N. But there had to be a way, Nina told herself, to change this unjust situation. Mark Danover could help. Dave Tolson would be invaluable, if he could just get past the barrier of Faye Calvert's hostility. And I can help, Nina decided.

One thing she knew when the day ended and she closed herself inside the luxuriously appointed room that was to be her new private sanctuary—Cindy Calvert was worth helping. Not only because she was a valuable human being who needed and deserved a life and a love of her own, but because Mark had arranged this job in the hope that a good friend, a woman in whom Cindy could confide, would make the necessary change.

For how could a nurse *not* want to do everything possible for a young patient who accepted a needle in her arm without flinching, thanked her nurse for 'going to so much trouble,' and then, smiling like the browbeaten, self-demeaning child that she was, say exactly what Nina hoped might be true: 'I think Mark's crazy about you. I've known him all my life, and I can *tell*. I think I'm going to write a poem about it. About

52

somebody being in love with somebody else and maybe not even knowing it.'

CHAPTER FOUR

If Cindy Calvert was living in a fantasy world, Nina's was painfully real.

One of the realities was discovering that Mark Danover, having found for his friend, patient, and neighbor a nurse that he could trust, busied himself elsewhere. Nina saw him for a brief, impersonal, doctor-nurse chat only once during the week that followed. He was satisfied that Cindy was in good hands. He had office appointments, rounds at two hospitals, hours scheduled for volunteer work at Community Day Clinic. Tired, he had nodded his approval of Nina's carefully kept chart, and rushed off before Mrs. Calvert could make an appearance in the living room. Nothing was said to imply that he had kissed Nina goodnight and that he had said, 'I more than like you.'

Disappointed, Nina had absorbed herself in the care of their patient. She had won unpleasant glances from Constance Bell for submitting a menu that had to be varied daily, depending on Cindy's physical activities.

'I've been cooking in this house for seven years,' the housekeeper had said tersely. 'I can follow a diet. I'm no dummy, you know.' Mrs. Bell had twisted her unsmiling face into a resentful scowl. 'The thing is, I'd like for you to decide what you want, Miss Bateman. If it's going to be different every day, I'll go out of my mind.'

'It *may* be different every day,' Nina had told her. 'It's going to depend upon how much energy Cindy burns up on a given day. And what her blood-sugar tests show.' She decided to try flattery, to win over the tight-lipped old harridan. 'You can't imagine how important a diet is to a diabetic patient.'

'I always managed before you came along,' Nina was told. 'I've been cooking for years and I've never had any complaints. Not until you started telling me how to run my kitchen.'

Nina tried, but failed, to hold her tongue. 'I'll keep you posted on what's needed,' she said. The imperious tone was irresistible. 'With all your experience, Mrs. Bell, you shouldn't have any problems.'

Constance Bell made a contemptuous sound and marched out of the kitchen.

Still recovering from the disturbing confrontation with the housekeeper, Nina ran into another obstacle with the maid twenty minutes later.

Leah had answered a ringing telephone. Preparing Cindy's injection, Nina had taken the refrigerated insulin from a lower shelf when the heavy-set, dopey-eyed domestic had taken a call on the kitchen telephone.

'No, she isn't,' Leah had said. A pause, and then, 'No. I'm sorry, she can't be disturbed.' Another silence, and then Leah was saying, 'I just told you she can't be disturbed. *'Sorry!'* The receiver had been dropped into its cradle with a click of finality.

It was obvious that the call couldn't have been for Faye Calvert; she had left the house an hour earlier with Ronald Perry. That left the inescapable conclusion that someone had tried to get in touch with Cindy and had been rebuffed. Something inside Nina rankled. 'Was that call for Cindy?' she asked.

'It wasn't for you, Miss.'

Nina ignored the sarcastic tone. 'If it was for Miss Calvert, she's in her room, wide awake. I think she should have been called to the phone.'

The blowsy woman in the black and white uniform gave Nina a withering look. 'When you start paying my salary, Miss Bateman, you can start giving me orders.'

'Was that . . .'

'I don't know who it was. That's not my business.' The maid fixed Nina with a watery, drunken stare. 'I got my orders, you got yours.' Leah made a big show out of gathering up a broom and dustpan from a service closet just outside the kitchen door. From the service porch, she said, 'I don't know about you, hon, but I'm workin' for Mrs. Calvert. When that changes, be sure an' let me know.'

It was in the angry mood imposed upon her by two inhuman lackeys that Nina conducted her after-lunch conversation with her patient.

'Gee, I wish Dave would call,' she heard Cindy saying. 'He *said* he'd call me this morning. Maybe he was too busy. Or maybe he's just getting tired of'—the girl hesitated—'I don't like to say this, but I know a couple of times I was taking a nap, or I was outdoors, and I guess Leah and Mrs. Bell were too busy to bother calling me. The next time I talked to Dave, he told me. And, after a while, when it's so hard to get away from classes to make a call, Dave could just give up.'

Cindy's misery demanded the question: 'Have you asked Leah or Mrs. Bell about that?'

'About my not being called to the phone?'

'Yes.'

'Oh, I've asked them, but you know how they are. They just mumble something and then they go back to whatever they were doing.'

Dissatisfied, Nina persisted. 'You don't suppose they have instructions, Cindy?'

'To keep Dave away from me? Even on the phone?' Cindy was close to tears. 'I guess I know that. I just . . . Mother's been so wonderful to me . . . I just don't like to say anything that'll upset her. I know she means well.'

'But you don't get annoyed? I'd be furious.'

Cindy looked at Nina as though she had uttered a blasphemy. 'When somebody cares as much about you as Mother cares about me? I couldn't. I mean, I'd just about fall to pieces if she got angry with me. And it would be like accusing somebody of . . . of . . . opening your mail.'

Except for the fact that Cindy was invariably at or near the front door when the mailman was due, Nina would have considered that possibility, too. Considering that there were telephone extensions all over the house, including one in the servants' quarters, it seemed unreasonable that there was no such instrument in Cindy's room. A teenager in a wealthy household would have demanded her own telephone, even if she hadn't been the only family member who was at home all day, every day.

Cindy's total lack of rebelliousness was unnatural. What girl her age would have tolerated this total, often deceitful control over her contact with other people? It was a form of dictatorship that only a weak, terribly confused young woman could have accepted. Furthermore, Cindy was so brainwashed into believing in her own helplessness, in her lack of judgment, and, conversely, in her mother's superiority, that she didn't object, even when she was anguished by the results.

'Cindy . . .' Nina wondered how to begin.

She had been hired as a nurse, not as a psychiatrist. Still, Mark had *said* that their patient should be living an active, normal life, within certain medical bounds that were not all that complicated. Tell her that it was Mrs. Calvert who had a mental problem? Shake the girl's confidence in someone who would be around long after Nina left? Nina tried a positive approach, avoiding mention of Mrs. Calvert. 'Honey, part of growing up is learning to stand on your own two feet. You're old enough and sensible enough to be trusted to make most of your own decisions. Deciding who's going to talk to you on the phone, or visit you, is . . . well, it's something you're able to do for yourself.'

Cindy responded with a hesitant half-nodding gesture, her eyes avoiding Nina's. 'A couple of times, I tried.'

'Try again,' Nina advised. 'And this time, be firm. You don't have to be afraid of creating a scene. Tell the help that you aren't a prisoner here. In fact, when your mother's out of the house, you're in *charge.* And that you want to be called to the phone, no matter *who* calls you.'

'Sometimes, when I know what time Dave's going to call, I'm right next to a phone, and . . .'

'That's something you shouldn't have to do. You're missing my point, Cindy. You have certain rights in your own home. There's nothing wrong with insisting that people respect those rights.'

'It'll get right back to Mother,' Cindy murmured. 'The other night, when you came here with Mark, I *did* insist that Dave be allowed to come in. The way it turned out, Mark brought him right into the room, so there wasn't anything Mother could do about it. But after Dave left . . .'

Nina didn't want to pry. Yet she was responsible for looking after her patient's emotional well-being as well as her physical condition. There was a relationship between the two, Nina reminded herself. 'What happened after Dave left?'

There was a heavy silence.

'All right, I won't pry, if you don't want to talk about it.'

'I *do* want to talk about it!' Nina was stunned by the vehemence of that cry. Cindy had crossed the room, dropping to the floor next to Nina's chair. Her thin hand closed over one of Nina's wrists, and she placed her head against her own hand, her shoulders shaking. 'I've *got* to talk about it! Nina, I know my mother loves me. She'd do anything in the world for me. I think about how many problems I've made for her and . . . it's just awful!'

'You haven't made problems for her, Cindy. Thousands and thousands of people are diabetic. They live useful lives. They go to work, follow careers, get married, raise families . . .'

'She's worried herself sick over me.' Cindy was getting her tears under control, but not her misery. 'She'd be free now. She'd be so happy, maybe getting married to Reverend Perry, doing the kind of spiritual work that means so much to her. But she's got me around her neck. I wasn't even up to facing a lot of people when she went to all that trouble, planning a debut for me. I would have felt so awkward and gawky, all those people staring at me and making a fuss over me. I just don't have Mother's poise. I'm just a dumb, sickly, helpless stringbean. And she has to spend her life worrying about me!'

Nina was incredulous. What years of conditioning it must have taken to convince Cindy that she was gawky, that she was incapable of looking after herself, making her own decisions! Convinced that she was inferior, Cindy had retreated to a romantic world of tragic poets with whom she could empathize and identify; her mother represented an ideal that she could not hope to reach—sure of herself, flashily attractive, quick-witted, and *strong*. And instead of stirring up resentment in the girl, Faye Calvert had convinced her daughter that she should be *grateful!* No wonder Mark had talked about an emotional problem in the Calvert household! Yet, if anyone who lived here was sick, it was

60

the woman who had made a bright, aesthetically lovely, completely lovable girl see herself as a burden—someone to be ashamed of.

Nina controlled her anger with Faye Calvert. Cindy was already wracked emotionally and this was no time to start trying to undo the damage that had been inflicted upon her during her formative years. *Later,* Nina thought grimly, later; gradually I'll start making Cindy believe in herself. She realized it would be hopeless to demand that Cindy assert herself right now. It had been a mistake to even make the suggestion. Build up her self-confidence. Smooth the path for her whenever possible. Set an example by being strong and firm herself. And tell Mark Danover how much *he* was needed as a buffer between Cindy and the enigma she loved and feared. Nina settled for tender, reassuring words, comforting her patient, then, with a show of busyness, getting her involved in a test that had to be taken, and, afterward, asking Cindy to read aloud the poems that she and Dave Tolson had exchanged.

Cindy's response was almost immediate. Like a child, she could be torn by sobs one moment and delight in sharing her daydreams the next. Yet it would be a mistake to go on treating her like an eight-year-old. Her mother was destroying her as a budding woman by doing exactly that. No, it would be a touchy job to keep Cindy as stable emotionally as injections of insulin kept her physically in balance.

It occurred to Nina, too, that part of Mrs. Calvert's determination to keep Cindy dependent on her was a desperate need to cling to her own fading youth. A tall, headstrong, self-sufficient daughter might have damaged the youthful image she struggled to maintain. But that didn't make sense, either—not when she strived so hard to force Cindy into a marriage to an older man. She was sick, Nina concluded. The woman might appear to have everything under control, but she was probably an emotional basket case. And if her motive, deliberate or subconscious, was to keep Cindy in a state of perpetual childhood, it was no doubt upsetting to look at the girl, to listen to her, and to realize that the child was enough of a woman to have fallen deeply in love.

Mark had said that the job would be a challenge. It was going to be that, all right. And not the least of doing what had to be done for Cindy Calvert involved avoiding a confrontation with her mother. It would have to come some day, Nina realized. But, until Cindy was strong enough to hold her own, it had to be delayed as long as possible.

Nina hadn't taken into consideration the fact that Faye Calvert thrived on confrontations. She had an insatiable need to throw her weight around, to establish her authority. And the clash came about not after a long period of preparation, but early that evening. The subject was a second telephone call from Dave Tolson.

Summoned to Mrs. Calvert's room for a 'private conference,' Nina knew in advance what was troubling the woman who was to pay her salary; she had seen Faye Calvert holding a whispered conference with Mrs. Bell minutes after she had returned to the house from the beauty salon.

Mrs. Calvert's private suite was located in a wing well separated from Cindy's room and Nina's. Minutes after the maid had said, 'Mrs. Calvert wants to talk to you,' Nina knocked on the door and was told to come inside.

Mrs. Calvert was seated at a white and gold antique dressing table, her back to Nina. Nor did she turn around. Wearing a flowing chiffon print dressing gown, her hair freshly coiffed, she was massaging her face with a thick white cream, her eyes fixed on the mirror before her. A cigarette burned in an ashtray on one side of the table; the other held a half-emptied martini glass, along with a staggering assortment of jars, tubes, vials, and perfume flacons. 'Close the door, please,' Nina was told.

'I don't have much time,' Mrs. Calvert went on in her superior tone. 'I have a dinner engagement with Ron . . . with Reverend Perry at eight. But I think there's something we should discuss, Miss Bateman.'

She didn't invite Nina to sit down, though the white-carpeted room was studded with enough brocade-upholstered chairs and lounges to make it qualify as a sixteenth-century salon. Nina stood near the door, aware that she was deliberately being made to feel awkward. She made a concentrated effort not to let Mrs. Calvert reduce her to the status of a serving maid who was going to be dressed down for some minor mistake. She lifted her head, took a deep breath, and reminded herself that she was a highly qualified professional, not Mrs. Calvert's lackey. 'What would you like to discuss, Mrs. Calvert?'

'If you're going to be employed here, I think we should define what your duties consist of.' The face-massaging process went on without interruption. 'You're here, Miss Bateman, to look after my daughter's physical well-being. I have Dr. Danover's word that you're quite capable in that area.' (Nina's nursing abilities were dismissed as carelessly as if Mrs. Calvert had complimented Leah on how well she had dusted the furniture.) 'But I think you should understand that I did *not* hire you to manage my personal affairs or those of my daughter. Nor are you to rescind orders that I give to other members of the household staff.'

'I don't consider myself a member of your household staff, Mrs. Calvert.'

The woman turned away from the mirror. Her face covered with the gooey cream, she looked like a clown wearing the first stage of his makeup. Nevertheless, she managed to sound superior. 'Oh? Oh, really.'

'I have a degree in nursing, Mrs. Calvert. I'm here at the recommendation of your daughter's physician. I'd like to be respected as a professional.'

Strangely, Nina's calm but uncompromising tone had a sobering effect on Mrs. Calvert. She sounded a bit less haughty as she said, 'You'll get all the respect you're entitled to, Miss Bateman. I appreciate your efforts. My point is that you've been here for a very short time. I've been responsible for Cindy all of her life. And I think I know what's best for her.'

Nina resisted the urge to disagree. 'If you're upset because I answered the telephone today . . .'

'I have every right to be upset. I pay Leah and Constance to take telephone messages when I'm not here. If a call comes for you, I'm sure you'll be called to the phone.'

'But Cindy won't.' The words had slipped out before Nina had a chance to judge their effect.

'There is a certain person whose calls are unwelcome here, Miss Bateman. As I told you a moment ago, I know what's good for Cindy and I intend to protect her from what is *not* good for her.'

65

It was too late to pretend polite innocence, 'Mrs. Calvert, Cindy happens to be very much in love with that "certain person." She's terribly lonely and a call from Dave Tolson does wonders for her morale. If she didn't have that to look forward to—'

'If she weren't wasting her time with a . . . low-class *nothing*—'

'He's studying to be a doctor, Mrs. Calvert! I don't see how you can—'

'It isn't your job to "see" anything!' Mrs. Calvert had gotten to her feet. Swiping at her face with a tissue, she faced Nina with a baleful look. 'As I was saying when you interrupted me, Miss Bateman, Cindy isn't mature enough to know a cheap young opportunist from someone who would be exactly right for her. You can't very well come into this house and think you know our family history. If you knew anything at all about my daughter, the way she's been brought up, the sort of people who *are* right for her, you wouldn't be presumptuous enough to stand there arguing with me. I simply won't tolerate arguments! I don't have to. When my daughter gets over this ridiculous starry-eyed infatuation, she'll thank me for guiding her in the right direction. And that direction, Miss Bateman, since you seem overly interested in personal matters which shouldn't concern you, is with a man who has already proven himself in the medical profession. I should think you'd

66

be impressed by that fact. A man whose background is of the same high level as that enjoyed by my daughter. Do I make myself clear?'

'But Cindy thinks of Dr. Danover as her . . . her father!'

'Well! You *have* overstepped your bounds, haven't you? May I remind you that you weren't brought here to discuss personal . . .'

'Cindy needs someone to talk to. Someone to confide in. And she must have told you how she feels!'

'She doesn't know any more about what's right for her than you do!' Faye Calvert's eyes blazed with anger. 'I don't think we're getting anywhere, Miss Bateman. Furthermore, I find your attitude . . .'

'Ask the doctor how *he* feels. Why he brought me here! He's worried about Cindy, but he's not in love with her. He's—'

Nina was unprepared for the shrill, ridiculing laugh. In spite of her elegantly dressed hair and the lovely gown she was wearing, Mrs. Calvert looked like a vindictive witch, ugly in her hatred. 'Oh, you are simply too ridiculous! You don't understand the first thing about the situation. Nor do I have any intention of explaining it to you.' The woman returned to her dressing table, staring at herself in the mirror as she removed the remainder of the white cream from her face. 'I should have expected that you might have some ambitions of your own. Nurses usually do, don't they? Find themselves secretly in love with the doctors they work for? It seems to me I've seen that situation on a few soap operas I had the misfortune to watch.'

If there had been any doubt in Nina's mind that Faye Calvert was emotionally unstable, that doubt was erased in the next instant. From the snobbish, ridiculing position she had taken, Cindy's mother made an instantaneous switch to playing the part of the all-seeing, understanding spiritual mentor. 'My dear, when you've studied as much as I have, *if* you were capable of understanding Reverend Perry's message, you'd know that we are all part of the Universal Whole. However, we each play our respective part in that great all-embracing consciousness. We try to *grow,* of course. Still, we have our assigned roles to play. And yours, Miss Bateman'—the harsh, demeaning tone had returned as quick as it had disappeared—'*yours*, Miss Bateman, is taking urine tests, seeing that my daughter's blood sugar is kept at a safe level, making certain that her diet is proper, and remembering that you are not a member of this family, nor are you here as a friend of this family. You're an employee. And, as an employee, I want it understood that you are not to contradict any orders I give to my housekeeper or my maid, and you are *not* to meddle in my daughter's private life. Do we understand each other *now?*'

Raging inside, Nina made one more attempt to reach the woman on a reasonable level. 'Mrs. Calvert, emotions play an important part in your daughter's illness. I know she's been miserable. This afternoon, chatting with someone who understands her and . . . and loves her, she was gloriously happy. No doctor or nurse or any medication could have done for her what that telephone call did. I'm not going to apologize to you for making it possible. If you have any doubt about Dave Tolson's importance to Cindy's health, you can talk to Dr. Danover.'

For a few seconds, looking at Mrs. Calvert's reflection in the mirror, Nina thought that the woman was going to explode. Her hands trembled, and her face had become a rigid mask. Then, just as Nina had decided that she had herself under control, Mrs. Calvert picked up a long-handled mirror and slammed it down on the dressing table. The martini glass toppled over the table edge, its contents spilling on the carpet. Leaping up once more, Faye Calvert shouted, 'I've heard all I want to hear!' She turned on Nina like an enraged wild-cat. 'I've heard enough to know that I don't want you around Cindy. I don't want you in this house. It's high time I learned not to lower myself . . . expose my own child to . . . to common, cheap, conniving . . .'

'You don't have to fire me,' Nina heard

herself crying out. 'I'll be happy to get out of your house!'

Someone was knocking on the door. Faye Calvert ignored the sound. Nina turned on her heels and walked toward the door, shaking with an anger that was equal to that of the older woman.

'Good. I'll have a new nurse here tomorrow morning! One who knows her place!'

'Be sure to tell Dr. Danover why you had to find someone else,' Nina called over her shoulder. She felt sorry for Cindy and dreaded telling her that the newly formed friendship was at an end. If there was one thing Cindy didn't need, it was an emotional upset. Nina opened the door, anxious to get away from a despicable woman and an ugly atmosphere.

She had forgotten that someone had been knocking on that door a few seconds earlier. She found herself face to face with Cindy.

The girl's face was drained of all color. She looked at Nina with wide-eyed shock. 'I knocked,' she said in a thin, croaking voice. 'Mother always wants me to knock . . . not just come barging in.'

'Come in, darling,' Mrs. Calvert invited. 'I had no idea it was you, dear. And I'd told Leah not to disturb me while I was getting ready to go out to dinner.'

'What's wrong?' Cindy looked from Nina to her mother and then back to Nina again. 'You were arguing. I couldn't help hearing you.

70

Something's wrong, isn't it?'

Nina lacked the heart to lie to her. Yet she was going to have to tell her that she was leaving.

Mrs. Calvert saved her the trouble. 'We've just reached an understanding, Cindy. Miss Bateman and I agreed that this isn't the sort of case she should be handling.'

Cindy made a stricken little cry, covering her mouth with her hands. 'Oh, no! No, please don't say that, Mother. Nina and I . . . Mother, I don't want her to go away. Not *ever!*'

Mrs. Calvert was in the doorway by that time, reeking of perfume and maternal concern. 'Honey, it's not the end of the world. Miss Bateman and I simply don't see eye to eye on some rather important subjects. We've decided, mutually, that . . .'

'You didn't ask *me!*' Cindy was crying, her wounded, anguished expression threatening hysteria. 'Neither of you! It's like . . . what I think . . . the way I feel doesn't matter to either one of you!' She looked accusingly at her mother and then at Nina. 'Mark's downstairs. I only came to tell you that.' She sobbed, then turned to run down the long hall that led to her room.

'Cindy, wait!' Nina started after her.

'She's my responsibility,' Mrs. Calvert said shortly. 'You may go downstairs and tell Dr. Danover that you're leaving. I hope you'll have the decency to tell him the truth about

71

why.'

'Cindy shouldn't be left alone,' Nina said. She had been dismissed; she had no right to follow Cindy to her room, yet she longed to soften the blow.

Perhaps Mrs. Calvert read her thoughts. 'You can say good-bye while you're packing your clothes. Cindy will get over it. She has a tendency to dramatize things, but she snaps out of it very quickly. Or writes one of those tragic little poems of hers.' Mrs. Calvert walked back into her room. 'Now, if you'll excuse me, I must start getting dressed. Tell the doctor that I'll see him before I leave. I'll arrange to have your check mailed to you.'

Torn between running after Cindy and trying to console her, and going downstairs to tell Mark what had happened, Nina followed neither course. Faye Calvert's callousness chilled her, then stirred her into a blind rage. 'You're a horrible person!' she cried out. 'You're the coldest, the cruelest, the most selfish excuse for a human being I've ever met!'

Nina's fury had exploded from her thoughtlessly. She had given no thought to the fact that her words might be heard down the corridor, that their effect on Cindy would be devastating. She had shouted out the truth, but she hadn't considered that someone other than Faye Calvert would hear what she had to say.

She heard Mrs. Calvert's shrill response: 'And you dare to call yourself a *nurse?*' The bedroom door was slammed, leaving Nina alone in the hallway.

She had started toward Cindy's room, concerned about the results of emotional turmoil in a diabetic patient. More than that, she wanted the girl to know that leaving hadn't been her idea; she had wanted to be more than a nurse; she had wanted, sincerely wanted, to be a friend.

As she neared the stairwell that bisected the two wings of the upper story, she heard Mark's voice: 'What's going on up there? Faye? Nina? What's happening?'

Mark Danover was at the foot of the stairway. As Nina came into his view, he called out to her again. 'Nina? Will you please come down here and tell me what's going on?'

Nina hesitated, looking down the thickly carpeted corridor to see that Cindy's door was closed. She would come and talk to Cindy in a few minutes, she decided. Mark had brought her to this house; he deserved an explanation.

When she reached the bottom of the steps, Mark made it clear that he had arrived at his own conclusion. 'I can't believe what I just heard, Nina. I wouldn't have imagined you were capable of talking that way to anyone, let alone someone who . . .'

'Someone who pays my salary?' Nina squared her shoulders. 'I've already been fired,

Doctor. I can express my feelings as an individual, and I just did!' She was facing him defiantly but Nina felt a tremor inside herself.

Mark looked more disappointed than shocked. 'You know what emotional scenes do to *any* kind of patient, especially a diabetic. You've been trained to control your temper. Frankly, I'm astounded. Name calling! It seems so beneath you.'

'You don't know what that woman's doing to Cindy. You don't know what she just said. Dismissed Cindy as though she were . . .'

'I *heard* Cindy,' Mark said evenly. 'She told me she'd let you know I was here. Next thing I knew, I heard her crying her heart out. What is going on?'

'Do you want my version, Doctor, or Mrs. Calvert's?' Nina felt uncomfortable under the searching stare. She felt defensive, persecuted, in need of striking back. 'I did what I think you would have done this afternoon. I made it possible for my patient to have contact with a human being who cares about her. Someone she loves.'

Mark frowned. 'Let's go into the living room.' He glanced up the stairs, as if he suspected either Cindy or her mother might be listening.

When they had seated themselves at the secretary desk where they had previously discussed Cindy's insulin therapy, Mark said, 'I presume you're talking about Dave Tolson. He called Cindy.'

'Yes. He's called repeatedly, and Mrs. Calvert's given orders to the help. Cindy isn't called to the phone and she isn't given any messages. I think it's the most inhuman . . .'

'Nina, our personal opinions aren't a part of our professional services. I may agree with you, but . . .'

'But you don't care how miserable that girl is. She's so pathetically lonely, and you told me yourself that there's no reason for it. She could be out having fun with other young people. I'd manage her diet and her insulin if she used up more energy. That was why I was hired, I thought. But she's living like a prisoner, for no reason. And if her mother took the time to try to compensate, to show a little compassion . . .'

'Nina?' Mark's eyes were sympathetic and critical at the same time. 'No personal opinions, remember?'

'All right, Doctor, I'll give you a professional opinion! Your patient isn't suffering from a disease; diabetes is a condition that can be controlled. But she's going through emotional trauma of the worst possible kind. She's living a totally unnatural life. And if there's anyone in this house who's sick, it's the person who's responsible for that. You told me there was an emotional problem here. You didn't tell me that Mrs. Calvert is . . .'

'Look, Nina, Cindy's a minor. No matter what you and I think, we can only recommend.

We can't dictate. And I would think that you'd know enough to use tact if you want something changed. Not shouted insults.'

Nina felt a rush of blood to her face. 'I'm sorry I blew up. If you'd heard the things she said . . . the way she brushed Cindy's misery off as though . . .'

Footsteps on the carpeted stairway were too well muffled to be heard, but the sound of Cindy's choking sobs cut Nina off in mid-sentence. 'Cindy,' she whispered. 'I don't want her to hear . . .'

Cindy ran into the room, tears streaming down her face. 'Tell her she can't leave, Mark. Oh, please! Tell Mother you don't want her to leave, either.'

Cindy had flung herself into the doctor's arms. She was almost as tall as Mark, but as he patted her shoulders comfortingly, the girl looked like a small child. 'Of course I don't want Nina to leave,' he said quietly. 'There's been a little misunderstanding. Now, if you'll just stay calm, maybe we can work it out.' Looking past Cindy, Mark's eyes pleaded with Nina not to contradict him. 'Nina and I were just about to go over your chart. How've you been feeling?'

'Since she's been here? You *know* I've been better.' Cindy was making a valiant effort to get her tears under control. 'She really cares about me, Mark. Just like you said; she really, truly cares. But that's not it. That's . . .'

'It's all right, Cindy. Believe me, everything's going to be all right.'

Mark's words were not heard. 'She *talks* to me,' Cindy was crying. 'She . . . she understands how I feel. So . . . so mixed up and . . . always wanting something . . . I don't even know what . . . and whatever it is, Mother thinks . . . she doesn't . . .'

Cindy was still being held in a fatherly embrace, still trying to articulate the confused feelings that drove her, so often, into an unreal world of gentle phrases, rhymed promises of love, soft words that spoke only of beauty, when the doorbell rang. There was a rustle of black taffeta and white organdy as the primly uniformed Mrs. Bell scurried by on her way to the door. Seconds later, the room was being invaded by two more people; Ronald Perry, immaculate in an elegant off-white suit and royal blue paisley Ascot tie, strolled in from one side, entering with the air of a man who is accustomed to dominating the scene. From the stairs, Faye Calvert, who had probably broken the world's record for applying makeup and getting dressed, swept in, probably concerned about what Nina might be saying to the doctor.

Mrs. Calvert and her handsome young spiritual adviser exchanged Hollywoodian embraces and she offered her face for a quick show-business peck on the cheek. She looked dazzling in a pale green silk cocktail dress. She exuded a heady, gardenia-based scent. And

77

there wasn't the faintest indication that a few minutes earlier she had been playing the natural part of a shrew. 'Darlings, I think you know each other,' she sang out. Her eyes swiftly took in Cindy, still held in Mark Danover's arms. She purred her satisfaction, ignoring her daughter's tear-streaked face. 'Oh, of course you do. You've all met.'

Nina felt awkward, wondering how fast she could excuse herself and go upstairs to pack without upsetting Cindy further.

'I'm early,' Ron Perry apologized. 'But if we're going to have dinner and get to the meeting on time, dear . . .'

'It's perfectly lovely,' Faye Calvert said. She beamed at Cindy. The girl was moving away from Mark, but the impact of seeing them close together had evidently buoyed Mrs. Calvert's spirits. 'I'm sure Mark and Cindy won't mind our running off. Evening free, Mark? None of those horrible hospital things that always keep you on the run?'

'I came to ask Cindy and her nurse to dinner,' Mark said evenly. 'I know it's a last-minute invitation, but Miss Proctor decided to treat me to home-cooked soul food and got carried away. There's enough for the Fifth Army.' He smiled at Cindy. 'If your dietician okays it, honey, you're coming next door for a fantastic meal.' The smile was turned on Nina. 'You'll have to do a calorie count, but that shouldn't take you too long.'

Mark's attempt to brighten the atmosphere failed. Nina tried, and failed, to return the light-hearted smile. Cindy had started toward the stairway, too dejected to make a reply. Suddenly she turned, addressing her mother. 'It's not true, is it? Nina isn't going away. I've just gotten . . . Mother, she . . . *if it was anybody's fault that I talked with Dave, it was mine!* And all we talked about was . . . how he's having trouble with this one Anatomy professor he has, and I asked if he ever read Shelley's "Lament," and then . . .'

'Darling, it isn't necessary to give me all the silly little details.' Faye released a tinny, artificial laugh. She seemed embarrassed, conscious of Mark's scrutiny, of Ronald's bored irritation with the tearful recital. 'Really. We'll talk about it later, dear.'

'But I don't want Nina . . . Miss Bateman to leave!' Cindy repeated. 'Mark, please tell her . . .'

'I think you and *I* ought to have a talk, Faye,' Mark said.

Mrs. Calvert's face flushed. 'Of course, Mark. Why not give me a jingle whenever you're free tomorrow? I'll be here most of the morning.' Ronald Perry was looking at his watch, adding to her sudden nervousness.

'I think you should take the time *now*,' Mark persisted. 'I don't have to tell you that Cindy's very upset. I'm speaking as her friend now. As her doctor, I was encouraged by the care she's been getting. I'm not at all pleased with the thought of Miss Bateman leaving the case.'

Cindy had started a fresh deluge of tears, turning away from the stiff gathering and making her way toward the stairs. 'If she leaves . . . I'll just want to die!'

Mrs. Calvert shook her head, muttering under her breath, 'That child should have been an actress. She thrives on melodrama.'

'She'd thrive better on friends,' Mark said. 'I can't tell you what to do about interested boyfriends, but she needs companionship. Every bit as much as she needs a conscientious nurse. Frankly, I can't accept responsibility unless I know she has the proper care. And neither you nor Mrs. Bell was providing it.'

Mrs. Calvert's hands touched at her coiffure. 'Well, if that's the way it's got to be. I suppose . . . possibly I was a little hasty. I agree with you. I think all three of us should have a little talk, so that Miss Bateman will understand my position. But not now, pet. We've really got to be running.'

'You're assuming that Miss Bateman will want to stay.' Mark glanced at Nina, then looked over to see that Cindy was standing near the foot of the steps, her hands clenched, her expression begging the people who had charge of her life to reach an accord. Nina's pride, her disgust with Mrs. Calvert, her urge to get away from this hateful woman, faded in a surge of compassion. 'Mrs. Calvert is right,' she said. 'I think we have some basic matters to discuss.' It was a noncommital statement; she had little hope that she could ever learn to live in the same house with Cindy's mother. But her words had a pacifying effect on Cindy. Mark nodded his approval. And Faye Calvert, taken off the hook, was free to link her arm through that of Ronald Perry and repeat that they simply had to run.

'Take good care of my baby,' Mrs. Calvert said as she started out of the room. Her escort, except for a heavy-lidded survey of Nina, made so subtly and swiftly that it escaped everyone else, didn't acknowledge the existence of anyone else by saying good night.

'She'll be right next door,' Mark said. 'Accompanied by her nurse and her doctor. I don't think you'll need to worry about her, Faye.'

'I'm sure it will be marvelous,' Mrs. Calvert said. She didn't wish Cindy a happy evening, only reminding her to be in bed at a sensible hour.

When the pair had left the house, Cindy hurried back across the room to hug Nina. 'You're going to stay! You've just *got* to stay.' Her tears were still not dry, but Cindy was childishly happy again. To Mark, she said, 'Is that really true? We're going to your house for dinner? The three of us?'

Mark chucked her under the chin. 'Miss Proctor doesn't know when to stop when she's cooking something she likes.' He grinned. 'She's gone so far overboard, I decided we'd better make it the four of us.'

For a few seconds, Cindy stared at him without comprehension. Then, as Mark's impish expression remained on his face, the meaning of his statement dawned on Cindy, as it did on Nina, and with a little cry of joy she threw her arms around the doctor and hugged him.

'I'm going home,' Mark said. 'You girls go upstairs and see what you can do about your puffy eyelids. But don't take any longer than fifteen minutes. Dave's due any second now.'

CHAPTER FIVE

Although Mavis Proctor, the Danover cook and housekeeper, had learned her culinary art as a child growing up in Alabama, the promised 'soul food' that evening reflected the soul of New England. A versatile cook, the scholarly looking black woman had taken Cindy's diet into consideration and prepared a dinner of corned beef and boiled vegetables. She had no objections to, and in fact welcomed Nina's pre-dinner visit to the kitchen.

'You mean you have to do this before every meal?' Miss Proctor wondered. 'All this weighing and counting grams and calories?' She made a clucking sound with her tongue. 'If I had to think about carbohydrates all day, I wouldn't get anything else done.'

'Fortunately, I don't have to do any cooking next door,' Nina said. 'But I manage to stay busy.'

'Doctor says he's real pleased. He used to worry about that poor child all the time.' Miss Proctor inspected a crystal wine glass to make sure it was spotless. 'I don't know how poor people manage. Or folks with just an average income. Somebody in that kind of income bracket can't pay for a full-time nurse.'

'They learn to do for themselves,' Nina told her. 'They learn to check their own blood sugar, give themselves injections, even regulate the dosage. And they learn what they can and can't eat. If they do something active, like, oh, going dancing, or enjoying some kind of sport, they know they've got to up their calories. They snack on fruit juice or milk or crackers . . . maybe a sandwich between meals. And they even learn what the doctor wants to know, so that he can decide whether they should be on fast-acting insulin or a slower type or a combination of the two.'

Mark came into the kitchen. 'What's this about telling what to the doctor?'

'I was just telling Miss Proctor that a lot of diabetic patients—in fact, most of them—learn how to care for themselves.'

'It's what I'm hoping you'll do for Cindy,' Mark said. 'When you're making tests, measuring an injection, explain what you're doing. She ought to be in here right now, learning the how and why of diet control.'

Nina laughed. 'Suppose I start the training when she doesn't have anything more interesting to do? Which is most of the time.'

Miss Proctor peeked out of the kitchen door. 'You just look at those two kids, Doctor. You think that little girl's going to be interested in how many grams of *anything* she's going to be allowed at the table?'

'Mavis, you're an incurable romantic,' Mark said. He turned his smile toward Nina. 'You know who introduced Cindy to Dave, don't you?' He thumbed at a proudly beaming cook. 'Miss Lonelyhearts, here. Dave was mowing our lawn and Cindy was out on the Calverts' back terrace reading. And, all of a sudden, something went click-click-click in Mave's head.'

'It was just plain logical,' Miss Proctor said. 'I'd been watching that pretty young thing sitting out there with a book, and just *nobody* to keep her company, week after week. Not to cast *aspersions,* but there's three ladies living in that house and there's not one of them would give anybody the time of day, let alone sit and visit. My stars, that child would light up like a Christmas tree every time I stopped by the hedge to make a little small talk. So here's this nice young man who's going to be a *doctor.*' The last word was pronounced with a hint of reverence. In spite of the easy camaraderie between Mark and the woman who kept his home going for him, Miss Proctor had a deep respect for his professional status. 'Here's this *fine* young man. I just said, "Miss Calvert, this is Mr. Tolson—who is going to be *Dr.* Tolson." It was the good Lord brought them next door to each other.'

'He has a way of doing that,' Mark said.

Perhaps it was an impersonal remark, but Nina felt a fluttering sensation inside. It was hard to believe that a short time ago she had been desperate to get into her car and to get as far away from this neighborhood as possible. Like Cindy, her mood had changed from one of torment to one of pure bliss. Maybe Mark was referring to her and to himself. If so, he didn't elaborate. It was enough just to be with him, enjoying the easy conversation, looking forward to a pleasant evening.

Mavis Proctor's lovingly prepared dinner may as well have consisted of boiled newspapers as far as Cindy Calvert was concerned. She raved about it, of course, making a huge fuss over everything that was being done for her, only emphasizing her loneliness by being so impressed with a simple social evening. But anyone watching her, anyone who knew her, saw that nothing mattered to Cindy except the fact that Dave

Tolson was seated beside her. The meeting of eyes, the 'accidental' brushing of hands, would have told a far less shrewd observer than Nina that Cindy was in love. Happily, her love was returned. Dave's ruddy face would grow ruddier at the brief contacts. They glowed, almost oblivious to the presence of friends who genuinely cared for them and had brought them together. And when Mark chided his housekeeper, telling Mavis Proctor that the only reason she liked Dave was because he had a giant appetite, Cindy's laughter was the sound of someone gloriously happy, *gloriously* in love.

After dinner, the young people accepted eagerly Mark's suggestion that they look over his library. 'I've never had time for much poetry since I left high school,' he said, 'but my dad has quite a few anthologies you might enjoy.'

Left alone with Mark, Nina sat edgily on the end of a long white modern sofa, wishing she could relax. Being with the man she loved, remembering the one brief kiss that had passed between them, she felt tense, wondering if he would bring up the subject of her tiff with Mrs. Calvert, and, if he did, what she would say. Cindy seemed to be taking it for granted that her nurse was not going to leave. Yet, the thought of another encounter with Faye Calvert . . .

Mark had apparently put that subject out of

his mind. Checking to see if Nina's wine glass was filled, and satisfying himself that it was, he said, 'Cindy's acting like this is a super gala—a big, exciting evening.'

'That's what it is for her,' Nina assured him. 'Can you even begin to imagine what it's like for a girl that age—a sharp, enthusiastic girl— to be living in that . . . gilded cage next door? It doesn't make sense to me. That anyone would impose that kind of life on her or that she'd accept it. But she's so browbeaten, so afraid of . . . I don't know what . . . of seeming ungrateful, she doesn't react like any seventeen-year-old I've ever known.'

'Cindy *isn't* like any seventeen-year-old you've ever known,' Mark said quietly. Animated voices from the small room set aside as a library reminded him that Cindy was not far away. 'Even before we discovered her diabetic condition, she was something of a loner. A dreamer. Faye had her wearing ten-year-old clothes when she was in high school. When she dropped out of school, she was treated like an invalid, made to feel like an invalid. She hasn't really grown up.'

Nina smiled, hearing laughter from the nearby room. 'She's getting there, Doctor.'

Mark smiled, too, understanding what she meant. 'I'm encouraging it. How'd you like the touch of sophistication at dinner?'

'Well, dietetically it was okay. Dry, white wine . . . one small glass. We both know that couldn't hurt her.'

'I liked the way she held the glass,' Mark said. 'She felt grown up. Woman-of-the-worldish.'

'I liked your touch,' Nina said. 'It was great for her morale. But, of course, the superb touch was arranging for Dave to be here tonight. She'll be honest with her mother, you know. She'll tell her Dave was here tonight and . . .'

'And you won't be blamed. I intend to have that long talk with Faye tomorrow.' Mark sipped from his wine glass thoughtfully before he spoke again. 'For one thing, she's going to be told in no uncertain terms that emotions play a serious role in diabetic regulation. When you leave, Nina, I want you to check Cindy's blood sugar. We might have to compensate for that upset tonight with extra insulin.'

'I really didn't plan on staying. But, of course, I wouldn't leave until you've found someone else . . .'

'I don't want someone else and neither does Cindy. Leave her mother to me, Nina. And try to understand that I can't alienate the woman. If I do, she'll take full charge of Cindy, and, God knows, neither of us would want that on our conscience.'

'I can't understand the woman. I can't guarantee I'll be able to get along with her.'

'Try,' Mark said. 'I've had an easier time

understanding her being hung up on that phony gigolo of hers because I was around when Faye was going through a lot of marital trauma. Cindy's father died when she was about three. I don't think she remembers him at all and neither do I, really. Then Faye married a guy some years her junior. She knocked herself out trying to stay young and trying to keep up with him. Apparently he had a roving eye. I know there were separations and reconciliations enough to keep a soap opera on the air for fifty seasons. And Cindy suffered from that. My mother used to tell me about it—how sorry she felt for the girl. They were together again when Lester was killed.'

'Tragic ending,' Nina said. She could think of no more profound comment to make.

'Well, *legally* together. Faye's husband was killed in his plane. On his way to Florida instead of the stockbrokers' convention he was supposed to be attending in New York.'

'Oh?'

'And he wasn't alone. His twenty-two-year-old secretary was killed in the crash with him.'

Nina thought about the situation for a moment. 'You'd think she would have learned to stay within her own age bracket.'

'Well, we know she hasn't. It's a desperate game, Nina. Frustrating and full of fears, probably. Not that it gives her the right to ruin Cindy's life, but . . . you get a glimmering of what motivates the woman from her past

89

experiences. It's, oh, the way I used to feel about Miss Proctor. Thought of her as a cold, dried up, loveless spinster. And then I got to know her and realized I shouldn't have leaped to conclusions. Mavis was going to marry a man who was killed in action during the Korean War. She's still comparatively young—in her early forties. But you couldn't begin to talk to her about making a new life for herself. We were rapping about falling in love with someone new after a tragedy like hers. One night I kept trying to convince her that while she couldn't *replace* the one big love in her life, there could be someone else. Someone different.'

'She's a very intelligent woman,' Nina said. 'She must know that.'

'Uh-uh. Know what she told me? "Once, when it's perfect, is more than anybody has a right to." So she works here, teaches Sunday school, sends money to a couple of nephews in Detroit, and lives vicariously. That's why she's so happy about how the kids have hit it off. And why she feels about Faye Calvert the way you must feel right now.'

'She was insulting,' Nina recalled. 'Belittling and insulting. And the next time Dave calls, if I'm near the telephone, I'm going to do exactly what I did this afternoon. Face it, I love Cindy and I'm concerned about her. But I'm not long for this job.'

'I understand how you feel,' Mark said. 'But

please stick it out, Nina. Without somebody with your sense of responsibility to look after Cindy, I'll be terribly worried.' He brightened. 'Besides, it's a joy to have you so close by.'

He would have elaborated on the subject, Nina was almost positive, but Cindy and Dave returned to the living room, holding hands, walking as though there were clouds under their feet. Mark noted Cindy's pallor and decided that she needed attention. An insulin boost, a snack, bed rest. Nina agreed, and the evening ended.

Mark walked them the few dozen yards to their door. Like Nina, he discreetly found something else to be doing while Dave kissed Cindy good night. The good-night kiss Nina longed for seemed inopportune, but she was left with the feeling that Mark had enjoyed being with her as much as she had delighted in being with him. If she could manage to stay on the job (and she would, if only because Mark had asked her to), there would be other evenings, and possibly some day . . .

She was still 'on duty' at nearly eleven that night, making sure that her ecstatic patient was as fit physically as she was romantically.

'It was so beautiful,' Cindy murmured as Nina started to leave her room. 'Three people who really, truly like me. *Love* me! Nina, this was . . . this had to be the happiest evening of my whole life.'

Nina smiled at the soulful, poetic sound of

the girl's voice, yet she was touched by it, too. Did Mrs. Calvert know, or care, how little it took to make her daughter happy?

Lying in her bed, sleepless as she reviewed the evening's progression from storm to calm, Nina realized that it hadn't taken much more to make herself ecstatically happy. She could think of improvements, but as long as she stayed here, there was the hope that the improvements would come about. It hadn't been *the* happiest evening in her life, but it had come close. Before sleep finally overtook her, she let the phrase drift through her mind repeatedly—it had come close.

CHAPTER SIX

Nina was not a part of the conference in which 'basic matters would be straightened out.' She was just as glad to be excluded from the long talk Mark had with Faye Calvert the next day. Nor did she learn what had been discussed or decided from Cindy's mother later that day. Mark, Nina guessed, would brief her when he found the time. In the meantime, Mrs. Calvert solved the confrontation problem by pretending that Nina didn't exist.

Except for the housekeeper and the maid, Cindy and Nina were alone in the house late that afternoon when she telephone rang. Leah was on the back terrace, talking with the gardener-handyman. Mrs. Bell was in her own quarters; a soap opera could be heard blaring from the direction of her room. And Cindy was taking a shower. Nina shrugged as she reached to pick up the telephone in the hall between the living and dining rooms. It was as good a time as any to test the new arrangement, if, indeed, any had been made.

Predictably, the call was from Dave Tolson. 'I'll get Cindy,' Nina said as soon as Dave had introduced himself. 'She's in the shower, though. Do you want to hang on, or shall I have her call you back?'

'She's never called me back,' Dave said. 'Mainly, I guess, because there's no place to call me.' Nina heard him laugh shortly. 'If you'll let her know I'm on, I think I'll wait.'

There was an excited whoop from the shower as Cindy was told who wanted to speak with her. Nina returned to the phone. 'Dave? She'll be here in just a few seconds.'

'Great. I can talk to you until then. Nice evening, huh?'

'Last night? It certainly was.'

'Cindy told me she was afraid you'd be quitting. She was really worried.'

'Did she tell you what it was all about?'

'Sure. I didn't get a chance to thank you last night. But I appreciate what you did. You're like Doc. One of the really super people. And, wow, if you think Cindy was anxious for you to

93

stay, you should have heard Doc. I talked to him alone for a few seconds before dinner and he's really gung-ho on keeping you right where you are.'

'Oh, really?' Nina had been told the same thing personally but it felt good to be hearing Mark's words again through a second party. 'What did he say?'

She had hoped for a repetition of Mark's praise for her as a nurse and as a person. Instead, Nina heard Dave telling her, 'I guess he's told you this. Doc wants somebody to keep an eye on that Perry guy. Ever hear his theories on how to get Cindy "cured" and off of insulin?'

'Just briefly,' Nina said. 'I know he doesn't think much of doctors and nurses.'

'Or medicine. Or surgery. Personally, I think it's just part of his gimmick. He teaches a course in some kind of mental control over illness. You know the racket—"You too can be rich, successful, popular, healthy." Lots of gullible people go for his kind of pitch. But I'll bet if he had a pain in his side, Perry'd be calling an M.D. in nothing flat.'

Nina was still waiting to hear what Mark had said about her. She needed a hopeful scrap of flattery to buoy her spirits. 'You were telling me what he said . . . what the doctor said . . .'

'About you? Yeah. For one thing, he bet me that Perry makes a pass at you.' Dave laughed a quick laugh. 'He's the kind of creep who thinks he's irresistible to women, so it helps that you're good-looking.'

Her spirits plummeting, Nina asked, 'What's that got to do with anything?'

'I don't really know. It's just a guess, but if Perry gets chummy with you, Mrs. Calvert might wise up and boot him out. In any case, once *you* get to know him, you'll know how he thinks and you'll be able to keep Doc posted.'

A bitter disappointment had risen in Nina. 'Posted on what?'

'On the phony ideas he tries to sell. Any off-beat medical treatments he tries to peddle to Mrs. Calvert. The doc is really fond of Cindy. And he knows he can trust you.'

Cindy, wrapped in a terrycloth robe, her hair bound in a huge towel, was hurrying toward the telephone. 'Here's Cindy,' Nina muttered. 'I'll . . . I'll see you, Dave.'

Cindy made an excited gesture as the receiver was handed to her. Nina walked toward her room, noticing as she neared the stairway that Constance Bell had positioned herself in the doorway between the kitchen and the dining room, straining to hear the telephone conversation. Perversely, Nina called out, 'It's all right, Mrs. Bell. The call is for *Cindy.*'

She was on the stairway and didn't see Mrs. Bell's reaction, but she gained some small satisfaction in knowing that she had irritated

95

the toady.

Once she had reached her room, the satisfaction was forgotten. Had Mark actually put her into this house to use her as bait? As a spy to observe Ronald Perry's actions? Was she expected to try to win the fake minister's confidence, then report her findings to Mark? Not that keeping an eye open for unorthodox 'medical' procedures wasn't a good idea, if Mark was convinced that Perry's influence represented a danger to his patient. But was being 'good-looking' one of the reasons she had been hired for this job? She felt shabby, suddenly, as though she were being used. Of course, Dave Tolson might have misunderstood Mark. Or, perhaps she was making more out of the casual, youthful chatter than was justified. But, somehow, there was no escaping the feeling that she had made a fool of herself in thinking Mark had chosen her to care for Cindy because she was an exceptional R.N., and because . . . because he wanted her living next door, wanted her near him, wanted to see her as often as possible.

Unpleasant thoughts were still rankling in Nina's head when the subject of that brief telephone discussion came to the Calvert house at four that afternoon. Cindy was in her room, either napping or daydreaming. Nina was checking her patient's insulin supply, which was kept in the kitchen refrigerator. She heard the doorbell ring, and was aware that

96

Leah had gone to the door. She was alone in the kitchen when Ronald Perry, more foppish than ever in a mod checked sports jacket and matching pale blue slacks, came into the kitchen.

'Well, hel-lo.' Ron's smile matched the overly personal expression in his eyes.

Nina responded with a casual 'hi,' replacing a vial on its special shelf.

'The maid tells me Faye isn't home yet. Know where she went?'

'No, I'm sorry. I'm surprised Leah didn't know. You might check with Mrs. Bell.'

'Didn't tell you where she was going?'

'I haven't spoken to Mrs. Calvert today,' Nina said.

'Beauty shop, probably,' Ron Perry guessed. There was a deprecating sound to his guess. If Nina had doubted that, he made it clear with his next sentence. 'Women that age spend a lot of time on facials and hair tinting. Part of our materialistic society, I'm afraid.'

Uncomfortable, Nina started out of the kitchen.

'In a rush? The hospitality of this house leaves a lot to be desired. If I'm going to have to wait around, you'd think somebody would offer me coffee.'

'I'll tell Mrs. Bell,' Nina said.

She found Ron Perry blocking her exit from the kitchen. 'Are you *that* busy? Really? I thought it was simply a matter of a few injections a day. Oh, and watching the diet. I believe Faye said you were big on diets.'

Nina summoned up her most contemptuous stare. 'Those "few injections" and the diet are what keep a diabetic patient alive, *"Reverend."* And diabetics happen to be more susceptible than you and I to high blood pressure, cardiac problems, eye and kidney blood vessel changes.' She felt foolish reciting the possible complications, knowing that her words were being wasted. The man was eyeing her with a look that was a cross between condescending amusement and wolfish interest. 'If you'll excuse me, please . . .'

'I was hoping we could talk a moment,' Nina was told in a tone that could only be called unctuous. (Interesting. Ron Perry was more than unusually attractive. He exuded sex appeal. Why did he have to work so hard at preserving that image?) 'I'm always fascinated by challenges, Nina.' Hastily, he added, 'Don't misunderstand me, please, dear. I mean *mental* challenges. I'm positive that if you were aware of more dynamic methods of helping the sick, you'd be a fantastic practitioner.'

'Being a nurse is good enough, thank you,' Nina told him.

'But can you visualize yourself as a nurse with tremendous, esoteric healing power? Material is an illusion, darling. What we call "matter" consists of imperceptible, constantly whirling atoms, subject to direction. Once you

98

uncover the secret wisdom of the ancient masters, matter will be something you can control!'

'I don't know enough about your subject to disagree with you,' Nina said. 'In the meantime, I'll have to stick to dull, surefire methods, like the use of insulin.'

'You *are* hostile,' Nina was told. 'But you're adorable when . . .'

'When I'm angry,' Nina said, finishing the sentence for him. 'I'm surprised at you. I thought that line went out with starched collars and the five-cent cup of coffee.'

Ron Perry brushed off the insult by laughing.

'We're going to have a long, long rap session one of these days. You intrigue me, dear.' More seriously, but still without moving out of Nina's way, he said, 'I wish I could prove what I'm trying to tell you. In fact, I could, just as I'm going to prove it to Faye one of these days. All medications are just a crutch. They're an acceptance of negative forces. And the most efficient way of disposing of negative force is to apply . . .'

'Positive force,' Nina cut in. 'In my patient's case, the positive force is knowing how to use Benedict's solution in testing for sugar, knowing . . .'

'You sound as stubborn as what's-his-name next door. Danover. And that totally brainwashed kid who drives Faye up the wall.

99

The funny young medical student.'

Nina gave him what she hoped was a scathing look. 'You know something? It was one of those "funny young medical students," a man named Charles Best, who helped Sir Frederick Banting prove that diabetics don't have to suffer and die. Before those two "funny" men gave us insulin, people like Cindy were doomed. Acidosis, coma, complications, dying young. That's what we had in the world until those two "materialists" made *their* dynamic discovery. I'm sorry, Mr. Perry, but I happen to have a deep respect for medical students. And not much fondness for people who put them down. Because, you see, they grow up to be the doctors we desperately need.'

'Marvelous! You-are-simply-marvelous!' The man was apparently impervious to insult. He had grasped Nina's shoulders and was staring at her with delighted approval: 'When you're convinced of something, you're a dramatic orator, love. You'd be a fantastic fund-raiser. Or evangelist! Oh, Nina, with your appearance and your presence of mind, your ability to articulate your thoughts, believe me, darling, your talents are being wasted. We'll have to get together and discuss . . .'

'Ron? I know you're here, darling . . . your car's in the driveway. But where . . .?'

Faye Calvert's voice, floating in from the entry hall, brought Ronald Perry's hands away from Nina's shoulders in the same instant that she was shaking herself free of the contact. He stepped aside, letting Nina pass. Nina was walking toward the stairway, feeling flushed and shaken, when she nearly collided with Mrs. Calvert.

There was a moment in which they both stopped, frozen in immobility. Mrs. Calvert looked beyond Nina to see her youthful spiritual adviser standing in the kitchen doorway. It didn't take her long to figure out that Nina had come from that direction. And Nina's unsettled feeling could not have helped. I almost *feel* guilty, Nina thought.

For a micro-instant, Faye Calvert's eyes bored into Nina's. Then, without a word or even a nod to acknowledge the nurse's presence, she swept on, her heavily made-up face assuming a theatrical smile of greeting and her voice taking on the sultry, purring quality that she affected in Ron Perry's presence. 'Oh, *there* you are, sweetness. What *are* you doing in the kitchen? Reduced to consorting with the help?'

Nina heard the woman's artificial laughter following her as she mounted the stairs. She felt cheapened and embarrassed. Ron Perry was annoying enough. Being all but caught in what must have appeared to be a cozy conversation with him was even more disturbing. But what upset Nina most was the vague realization that Mark Danover *wanted* her to encourage the man's attentions. To make Faye Calvert jealous? To get Perry to reveal the anti-medical philosophy that Mrs. Calvert was buying hook, line, and sinker? No, Mark would have told her that if this was his intention in hiring her. But would he have, really? The whole idea smacked of melodrama, intrigue, and unethical practice.

Nina spent the evening in Cindy's room, exchanging confidences, trying to dismiss the upsetting thoughts from her mind. (Dave had misunderstood. Mark would assure her of that the next time they talked.)

According to Mavis Proctor, who telephoned to tell Cindy that one of her favorite contemporary poets was going to be on a talk show at eleven that night, Dr. Danover was at the hospital, called in on an emergency, and wasn't expected until late. There was no hope of hearing from him that night.

Nina watched the television program with her dreamy-eyed patient, fixed Cindy a late-night snack, and went to her room near midnight, half wishing that she was back at Community Day Clinic. But only *half* wishing. Just the hope of seeing Mark Danover again, the almost sure knowledge that she would see him the next day, would keep her on this case as long as Mark wanted her here.

CHAPTER SEVEN

It wasn't necessary to avoid Mrs. Calvert during the next two weeks. Cindy's mother was devoting herself with zealous dedication to a new membership drive that would make Ronald Perry's new Temple of Universal Wisdom a monetary success. She had put up the money for a mail campaign and for nationwide advertisements. From the few snatches of conversation on the subject that Nina heard around the house, the object was to develop a mailing list for selling a course in the Reverend Perry's mind-over-matter techniques. There was talk about constructing a permanent temple, with adjacent living quarters for the spiritual leader. Mrs. Calvert was too busy, too engrossed, to bother about her daughter's nurse or for that matter, her daughter.

Cindy took advantage of the situation by enjoying long telephone conversations with Dave Tolson. When Dave could spare an evening from his studies, he made his way to the Calvert home. Nina would make a discreet disappearance, emerging from her room only when Dave stayed on too late and Mrs. Calvert was due home. If Cindy told her mother about the visits (and Nina was sure that she did), no issue was made of the matter. Apparently

Mark had gotten across the importance of avoiding emotional scenes with his young patient. Certainly, Mrs. Bell reported the calls from Dave Tolson. Nina was not called on the carpet again.

As her friendship with Cindy grew, Nina found that most of their conversations centered around Dave. Mark was seldom mentioned, probably because his checkup visits were brief. He had taken on, in addition to his private practice and his volunteer work at the clinic, a staff assignment at a new doctor-owned hospital. He was active in medical associations, he was one of the rare medics who did not rule out all house calls, and there were three or four evenings each week when he was called to one hospital or another in emergencies. Nina did not see him, except in Cindy's company, or when Mrs. Calvert and her servants were hovering nearby. Discouraged, she began to wonder if Dave's guess as to why she had been hired was not accurate. More than that, she castigated herself for having been a romantic fool. One impulsive kiss had hardly committed the doctor to a serious interest in her. Mark lived in a world far removed from her own.

One weekend, driving to her old neighborhood to visit her mother, Nina experienced an almost nostalgic feeling for home. She was, and always would be, a stranger in the Calvert household, in spite of

Cindy's warm regard for her. Mark probably saw her as an outsider, too. Busy, on the run, he discussed Cindy's regimen with Nina, apologized for having to hurry off, and after expressing satisfaction with the job Nina was doing, rushed to his next appointment. There was neither the time, nor the inclination on Nina's part, to question him about his reason for putting her on the case. The words that had disturbed her seemed vague and ephemeral; she would have felt embarrassed to mention Ronald Perry or her possible attractiveness to Mrs. Calvert's ambitious young boyfriend.

'I think Mother's decided Dave's not a monster, after all,' Cindy said one afternoon. 'She knows he's been coming over when she's not here. And she hasn't said one word to me about it.'

Cindy seemed too happy to be disturbed by an analysis of why her mother wasn't objecting to Dave's visits. Nina's guess was that the woman was, *A.*, too busy with her own hectic romance to worry about anything else, and, *B.*, convinced that if she ignored the penniless young medical student long enough, Cindy would tire of him. And, apparently Mark had made his point; emotional upsets constituted a danger to Cindy's well-being. Faye Calvert was being inordinately cool.

Nina should have guessed that a woman as domineering as Mrs. Calvert wouldn't accept the situation gracefully for long. She reverted to type one evening when Cindy and Dave had decided that the spring evening was meant for walking, preferably hand in hand. Nina had seen no reason why they shouldn't do so. They were out of the house when Mrs. Calvert's Lincoln purred up the driveway.

It was only Nina's guess, but it seemed that something had gone wrong between Faye Calvert and Ronald Perry. She stamped into the house, her face contorted with anger.

Nina was in the process of carrying a snack to Cindy's room; after the unaccustomed exertion of a walk, she would need a bedtime energy boost. Mrs. Calvert's question stopped Nina near the foot of the stairway. 'Is my daughter in her room?' She nodded at the tray Nina was carrying. 'If she is, tell her I'll be up in a few minutes. Soon as I fix myself a drink.'

'Cindy's not in her room,' Nina said.

Mrs. Calvert drew nearer, her hazel eyes cold and questioning. 'Oh?'

'She's gone for a walk.'

'Alone? It's dark out. You ought to know better than to . . .'

'She's quite safe,' Nina said with a nonchalance she did not feel. 'She's with Dave Tolson.'

Mrs. Calvert glared at Nina, then at the tray in Nina's hand. She seemed to be controlling her temper with effort. Nina waited for the explosion, but nothing more was said. Mrs.

Calvert walked to the liquor cabinet. As Nina started up the steps, she heard the front door open. Laughing voices announced that Cindy and Dave had returned.

Nina paused on the stairway, listening. She heard Mrs. Calvert say, 'Cindy, I'm terribly disappointed in you. You know that you aren't supposed to exert yourself.'

'I'm allowed all the exercise I want,' Cindy protested. 'Ask Mark. Ask Nina. They just compensate for the calories I burn up by . . .'

'I don't need a clinical report, darling. What I'm saying is that I don't want you roaming around at night, tiring yourself out. Especially not in the company of someone you know I don't approve of.'

'I'm sorry you don't approve of me, Mrs. Calvert.' Dave's voice had a strong and steady resonance. 'I'd like you to know that I wouldn't do anything that . . .'

'Cindy, do I *have* to listen to this? I think I've made myself clear. I've been patient. My patience with you, your "friend," and the nurse who's supposed to be looking out after you is just about exhausted.'

Nina hated herself for eavesdropping, yet she remained fixed in her spot on the stairway. In another minute, she was certain, Cindy would burst into tears.

Nina's expectation was wrong. She could hardly believe her ears when she heard the girl say, 'Mother, I don't think that's any way to talk about Miss Bateman. She's been wonderful to me. I've been feeling better than . . .'

'She's been doing what I pay her to do.' Mrs. Calvert's voice had a sharp edge. 'Except for letting you go out tramping around with . . .'

'And I don't think you ought to talk about Dave that way, either.'

Nina listened, the tray unsteady in her hands, unable to believe what she was hearing.

'He's my friend. He's a . . . guest in our house. I wouldn't talk to one of *your* friends that way.'

There was no response from Cindy's mother. Perhaps she was too shocked by Cindy's sudden rush of strength. It was polite defiance, but defiance, nevertheless. Dave must be staring at Cindy with disbelief, Nina guessed.

'No, that's not right,' Cindy went on. 'He's *not* just my friend. Dave loves me, Mother, I love *him*.'

There was a furious, choking sound from Mrs. Calvert. 'Cindy, I don't want another big emotional scene, but this is ridiculous! Young man, I think I've had all I want of your bad influence and Miss Bateman's. I'll thank you to leave this house while I'm . . .'

'He doesn't have to leave this house!' Cindy's cry echoed through the living room, penetrating the stairwell. 'I have my rights, Mother. In . . . in just a few months I'll be eighteen. I won't have to do every single thing you tell me to do! I'll be able to have any friends I want!'

Her voice shaky, Mrs. Calvert responded to the unusual outburst with a cold high-handedness that bordered on the vicious. 'Your friend, here, might be interested in knowing that you won't come into your inheritance until you're twenty-one. He might be slightly put off if I told him what your medical expenses will run between then and now.'

'Mrs. Calvert—'

Dave's protest was drowned out by a shrill cry from Cindy. 'He wouldn't care! He loves me, and he wouldn't care! You think that's all anybody cares about, Mother? Just . . . *money?* Maybe that's what Ron Perry thinks about, but not Dave. I told you he *loves* me. And if you won't let him come here . . . if you don't talk to him like . . . like somebody who means a lot to me, I'll . . . I'll leave. I will! I don't want to, but I'll get out of this house and go away with him.'

'Hey, easy, Cindy.'

Dave's calming words were ignored. 'I mean that, Mother.' Cindy's voice broke with emotion, but she persisted. 'I've never argued with you before. Maybe it's because I . . . not just because I love you, but . . . because I never cared about anything or . . . anybody.'

Mrs. Calvert's voice was controlled but grim. 'You sound very tired, Cindy. We'll talk about it in the morning.'

'I won't feel any differently in the morning,' Cindy warned. But her tone had lost its aggressive quality. She sounded meek and timid, her words barely audible to Nina.

'I'll call you tomorrow,' Nina heard Dave promise. He said, 'Good night, Mrs. Calvert.' But there was no response.

Nina continued up the stairs, setting the tray with milk and crackers on it next to Cindy's bed, then went to her own room.

A short time later, Cindy came upstairs. Nina returned to the girl's room, concerned about how the radical outburst had affected her. Cindy was amazingly calm. 'Did you hear?' she whispered.

Nina nodded. 'I didn't mean to. But, yes. Yes, I did.'

'Mother's awfully shook up. I think she was shook up before I came in with Dave. I can always tell when something's gone wrong for her. And I hated to . . . you know, say the things I did.'

'They were honest,' Nina told her. 'I was proud of you, Cindy.'

Cindy had dropped to the edge of her bed. 'I surprised myself. The thing is, I feel so crummy about it, Nina. Why can't she just accept Dave . . .' She released a long sigh. 'She was sitting in the living room when I came up here. Not crying, but I could tell she was going to.'

'Drink your milk,' Nina advised. 'And get some sleep. We'll have to check you out first thing in the morning. You haven't gone for a walk in ages, have you? We'll have to compensate.'

'And tomorrow morning, I want you to show me *how* I compensate,' Cindy said. 'I mean, if Dave and I . . . well, we can't get married now. He won't have any money for ages and I won't have any of my own until I'm twenty-one. But if we *should* get married, I know he wouldn't be able to afford a nurse for me. I'd have to do the whole insulin bit myself, wouldn't I?'

'I guess you would, Cindy.' Nina felt as though she was watching a girl grow up into a responsible woman before her eyes. 'It's not that complicated, once you get used to it. And Mark wants you to learn to take care of yourself.'

Cindy picked up a cracker, nibbling on it absently. 'Just before I came upstairs, Mother said something to me about Mark. About how we've always been so close and about how stupid I'd be to marry anyone else. Poor thing. She can be so smart in some ways and so naïve in others. Anybody who knows anything about Mark knows he's'—Cindy hesitated—'knows he's so wrapped up in his work, maybe still getting over that girl he broke up with four years ago, that he's just not . . .' Cindy looked up at Nina helplessly. 'I hate to say this, but . . .'

'He's not in love with anybody,' Nina said.

Cindy nodded miserably. 'I thought he might be. I think he's out of his mind not to be.' Her dark eyes found Nina's, looking at her almost apologetically. 'It's awful to be this happy, this *loved*, and not to have everybody around you feeling the same way. Mother. You. I just wish everybody in the world could be as lucky as I am!'

CHAPTER EIGHT

With Dave Tolson's words, and then Cindy's, still ringing in her consciousness, Nina was only professionally pleasant when Mark came across the lawn the next evening to give Cindy a check-up.

Cindy was due for an injection and she decided that she wanted her doctor to see what she had learned that morning about withdrawing thirty units of regular insulin and fifteen units of the long-acting type into a syringe, her first step toward the self-care that had now become so important to her. Nina left the bedroom, going downstairs for the insulin bottles.

Mrs. Calvert's voice, somewhat high-pitched and agitated, was heard from the drawing room. She had been at home all day, sleeping until nearly two, then pacing around the house, finding fault with everything Leah and Mrs. Bell did, acting as though Nina were beneath her notice, and talking to Cindy only briefly about the girl's need for a new summer wardrobe. She was on the telephone now, apparently talking with Ron Perry, because Nina heard her say, 'But I *do* believe you, darling. It's not as easy as you think for me to practice what you preach. The man's been a friend and neighbor for years and he *has* managed to keep Cindy in reasonably good shape, considering.' There was a short pause as Nina crossed the living room, an unwilling eavesdropper. Then Mrs. Calvert cried, 'Dear, I *know* it's bad for your image, but no one knows I have a daughter under conventional medical care. It's not as though one of your flock is going to come here and check out my faith in you. And, besides, you know I have personal reasons for tolerating the status quo. I'm sure the two of them will realize how right they are for each other, sooner or later. Do you think I'd be putting up with what I'm going through if I didn't believe that? Darling, please be patient. If I make any radical changes now, she's liable to run off with that absurd thing with the freckles, and you know what that's going to mean financially. Let's kiss and make up, love, and I'll drive up to see you tonight. Isn't that what we both want, Ronnie? Just the two of us, our mission together . . . ?

Mrs. Calvert's voice drifted off as Nina

reached the kitchen. Puzzling over the strange words, Nina was preparing a syringe for sterilization when Mrs. Calvert came into the kitchen. She looked blowsy and breathless, glancing around the room irritably and saying, 'Any time you want a cup of coffee or a drink, you can count on Constance to be in her room and Leah to have the evening off.'

For someone else equally helpless, Nina would have offered to fix coffee. Perversely, she remained at the sink, rinsing the syringe and needle with cold water. It was petty, perhaps; it would have been just as easy to prepare coffee while she waited for the saucepan of water to start boiling on the stove. But there was a small measure of satisfaction in not allowing Faye Calvert to reduce her to a menial lackey.

Since coffee was too complicated to prepare, Mrs. Calvert left the kitchen and returned shortly afterward with a filled brandy snifter in her hand. There was nothing for her to do in the kitchen; it was rare for her to enter the room. Leaning against one of the tiled counters, she asked abruptly, 'Is the doctor still here?'

'Yes. He's in Cindy's room.'

Nina turned to see bleary, disparaging eyes viewing the pot of water. As Nina placed the barrel and plunger into the water, Mrs. Calvert said, 'You people really do go through a lot of impressive ceremonies.' She picked up a bottle of aqueous Zephiran that Nina had ready to place on a tray. 'This some more of the poison you're injecting into that poor baby?'

Nina drew in her breath and held it for several seconds before daring to reply. 'That's a disinfectant, Mrs. Calvert. It's used to rub the cap of the insulin bottle.'

Mrs. Calvert shook her head back and forth slowly. 'Archaic,' she muttered. 'When a complete cure is so readily available.'

'We wish that were so,' Nina said. She realized that the woman wasn't downing her first drink of the day. Arguing with her when she was sober was bad enough; catching her in her cups and in a frustrated mood called for heroic self-restraint. 'Unfortunately, all we can do is . . .'

'Use people as guinea pigs and prolong their misery.'

It would be ten minutes before she could escape. Nina glanced at her watch, trying to rise above the ignorance and the insults to the medical profession. Why was the woman here? Was she deliberately trying to provoke a scene? *Say nothing,* Nina decided. She started preparing the tray she would carry to Cindy's room, determined to avoid a quarrel.

Mrs. Calvert fished a cigarette from the pocket of a svelte black 'at home' lounging ensemble. Lighting up, she said, 'I suppose you know I wasn't pleased with what happened last night?'

115

'The walk? It was good for Cindy. She's needed more exercise—a better appetite. And I took the extra activity into account when I measured ...'

'Not simply the walk. Although you certainly knew how I'd feel about her going out without my knowledge. The company, Miss Bateman. In a weak moment, I let myself be talked into giving my daughter more leeway, but it's obvious to me that she's too immature to handle responsibility for herself. She's too young and naïve to know that there are thousands of people in this world looking for a way to step upward. That Tolson boy ...'

'He's definitely looking for a way up,' Nina conceded. 'So much so, that he's working day and night to get a medical education.'

Nina's sarcasm eluded Mrs. Calvert. 'I think we've covered this subject before. I have a right to protect my daughter from trash. No family background, no breeding, no resources. I'm surprised you aren't encouraging Cindy to think she's madly in love with Pike.' Before Nina could respond, Mrs. Calvert downed a quick swallow of brandy and said, 'Of course, it's becoming rather obvious why you're so cooperative in letting Cindy think about ruining her life.'

'Ruin her ... ?'

'You know perfectly well what I'm talking about, Miss Bateman, so please don't feign innocence.' It was amazing how the woman could teeter on her spike-heeled mules as she leaned on the counter, yet managed to keep from slurring a single syllable. Her words had the sharp, clipped stacatto of a typewriter. 'You know what I want for my daughter. She's too young to know what's good for her. And Mark Danover is still getting over a silly infatuation with some . . . nurse.' The last word was pronounced with scathing emphasis, as though it were a crowning insult. 'But I've known for two years that it's simply a matter of time before they both realize they're right for each other.'

Nina started to contradict her, but thought better of it. She glanced at her watch again, longing for the boiling time to pass, thinking about leaving the kitchen and coming back later.

'And, as I was saying, it's become rather apparent why you're promoting this absurd relationship between Cindy and that nobody. Acquisitive people are so transparent, Miss Bateman. I find your designs on Mark Danover somewhat pitiful. You must know you're aiming way over your head.'

Nina cursed herself for turning red. She didn't have to look into a mirror to know that her face had colored, that she looked embarrassed. Her words barely audible, Nina said, 'I don't think I have to discuss my personal life with you, Mrs. Calvert. Or how I happen to feel about . . . anyone.'

Mrs. Calvert made an attempt to draw herself up into a haughty, commanding pose. She failed, but her voice conveyed the same effect. 'I'm not even faintly interested in your personal life. Except when it has an effect upon mine. Cindy's future, that's all I'm concerned about. You've managed to get next to her and I'm not looking forward to another of her tantrums about being torn away from you. Since I seem to be stuck with a tacky situation, I'd like to have a . . . civilized understanding. What I want you to know, Miss Bateman, is that I'm aware of your . . . motivation. I think it's unfortunate, but you can't deny that you're in love with Mark.'

It would have been easy to make the denial. But some of Cindy's newly found rebellion had transferred itself to Nina. She felt furious, tired of being belittled professionally and now personally. In a burst of defiance, Nina cried, 'What business is it of yours? What if I am? All right, I'll admit it! I respect him, I admire him, I love him! That has nothing to do with . . .'

'It has everything to do with the matter!' Mrs. Calvert shrilled. 'Now that I know you can't be trusted, I can't wait for you to get out of my house!'

'Don't you know a watched pot never boils?'

Mark's voice, from somewhere near the kitchen door, stopped Nina from announcing that *she* couldn't wait to get out of Mrs. Calvert's house. If Cindy had come downstairs

118

with her doctor, there would be another big emotional disturbance, unsettling to everyone else, dangerous to Cindy.

Mrs. Calvert was either too drunk or too indifferent to hold her tongue. 'That's all I wanted from you, Miss Bateman. Your admission that you're in love with Cindy's doctor.'

Mark had walked up to the kitchen door, stopping in his tracks at the mention of his name.

He was unnoticed by Mrs. Calvert. 'You'd be wise to get out before he finds out why you're here and why you're encouraging my daughter to wreck her whole future!'

'That isn't true and you know it!' Nina heard herself protesting. She turned to Mark, anger and humiliation bringing tears to her eyes. 'Doctor, I don't want another big scene. Is Cindy with you?'

Mark shook his head slowly. 'No, she's waiting upstairs.' He looked dismayed and bewildered. 'What's wrong now?'

Faye Calvert had become aware of her audience. This time she managed a semblance of poise—poise and a soft, controlled tone that would invite sympathy. 'I don't want to burden you with my personal troubles, Mark. I don't want to go back on our . . . agreement, but . . .' She sighed, martyrlike. then made her way out of the kitchen, looking touchingly forlorn and leaving the not-yet-emptied brandy snifter

119

behind her on the kitchen counter. 'I'm not up to talking now.'

Nina concentrated on the boiling water, wishing she had better control over her tears. She blinked them back, turning so that Mark could not see her face.

'What was *that* all about?' Mark demanded.

'Maybe I'm not up to talking about it now, either,' Nina said. Her hands trembled as she removed a ball of cotton from its blue carton with tweezers.

Mark was solemn. 'I'm afraid we're going to have to talk about it, Nina. I had no idea the situation would get this tense. It's not good for you. It's apparently driving Faye to drink. At least more so than usual. But my main concern has got to be with Cindy.'

'I thought I've been doing a rather good job in that department,' Nina said. Dave Tolson's words flashed in her mind; she felt used and unappreciated.

'You have,' Mark said quietly. 'You have. But I'd hoped you'd be able to get along with Mrs. Calvert. You've studied psych. You know something about handling difficult people, neurotics. And twice now I've heard you haggling like fish-wives. You're a *nurse!*'

Nina gave up trying to hold back her tears. 'I'm a human being, too!' she protested hotly. 'But maybe that hasn't occurred to you.' She turned away from the stove area, walking toward the refrigerator, feeling ridiculous

120

because there was no reason for her to be standing there with her legs shaking. Her humiliation could only be covered by a resentful attack. 'You've always managed to hear the tail end of a conversation. You haven't heard what Mrs. Calvert says about . . .'

'About you?' There was a terrible silence. 'About me? This isn't an ethical conversation, Nina. A doctor and a nurse don't discuss the patient's family unless there's something constructive . . .'

'About your profession and mine!' Nina cried. 'About the "stupidity" of what we're trying to do for Cindy! And about me . . . as a person! I've had it, Doctor. Cindy's found somebody who loves her enough so that she'll manage without my companionship. All she needs is a competent nurse who'll teach her what I've started teaching her. How to take care of herself and *free* herself from the sickest, greediest, most vicious . . .'

'You as a person,' Mark said softly. 'That's the part I want to hear about. What I heard Faye saying when I came in here.' He paused for a moment. 'I apologize for what I said about ethics. And I believe you, Nina. What I'd like to believe . . .'

Nina swiped at the top of an insulin bottle with the disinfectant-soaked ball of cotton. It was a savage move. 'You can believe anything you want. I'm through here.'

Mark had moved closer to her. His hands fell on her shoulders, gently turning Nina around to face him. She kept her eyes cast downward. 'I only heard it from Faye,' Mark said. 'If it's true, I'd rather hear it from you.'

She was too disturbed for game-playing or coyness. 'That I love you? I'm not ashamed of that. What if I do? I haven't asked anything from you . . . expected anything from you. There isn't anything I can do about that. There's nothing you can do, Mark. I was in love with you a long time before I came to this house.'

Mark's right hand left her shoulder, his index finger lifting Nina's chin, forcing her to look at him. 'Nina.' He pronounced her name gently, like a benediction. 'Nina! You were always so cool, so reserved. I couldn't imagine . . .'

Mark's arms had closed around her. He was kissing her then, not with the casual friendliness that had been inherent in that first kiss (only weeks ago, though it seemed that years had gone by) but with the fervor and hunger a man denotes when he kisses a woman he loves. *Loves and wants!* Nina's tears had not dried, but she forgot the ugly scene that had made this moment possible. As Mark's lips held fast to hers, she lifted her arms, encircling his neck, feeling his embrace tighten.

They remained locked in that embrace. for a long time, though it seemed to Nina that it could never be long enough, close enough. When Mark freed her, his voice was husky with emotion. 'Why were you always so distant? I thought . . . someone so beautiful . . . you couldn't possibly care about me.'

Shaken by a flood of new emotions, Nina tried to busy herself preparing the tray. 'Don't you think I wasn't aware of all the things Mrs. Calvert talks about? I *live* in the neighborhood where you do your charitable work, Mark. I've never been inside a country club. My mother never headed an opera committee or chose the debutantes for a coming-out party. My mother checks groceries in a supermarket. Your whole world . . . you were someone I—'

He had closed the distance between them again, taking Nina back into his arms. 'Are you really still bound up in that "different worlds" thing? Darling, don't you know that nobody thinks that way anymore? God knows, I never did.'

Nina found herself clinging to him, her eyes pressed shut. 'Mrs. Calvert does. She keeps reminding me.'

'Mrs. Calvert!' Mark almost spat out the name. 'She doesn't know the first thing about love. Cindy's for Dave, yours for me, mine for you.'

He was kissing Nina repeatedly, then, telling her over and over that he loved her. 'Almost from the start, Nina. But I'd had this . . . ridiculous experience. Somebody I thought I

123

loved. One of those collectors who wants exclusive rights to you. And thinks she has the right to be nationally syndicated.' Mark laughed, suddenly, at his own metaphor. 'My parents were fairly sophisticated as far as the outside world was concerned. But between them, they were terribly old-fashioned. Wonderfully old-fashioned, Nina. I think it rubbed off on me. I've spent most of my adult years looking for somebody who believes—' He moved Nina away from him, tenderly, so that he could look into her eyes once again. 'Somebody who believes that love is a very exclusive thing. Two people, one commitment. That's the way I love you, Nina. I still can't get over . . . your caring for me the same way.'

She wasn't dreaming. Mark was actually saying words that she had never really hoped to hear. His body, pressed close to her own was warm and real. It was the impossible happening, and Nina felt like crying again, this time possessed by a surge of love and gratitude and astonishment so overwhelming that she could find no words to express herself.

There seemed to be no further need for words. Mark was kissing her forehead, her eyes, her cheek, then locking his mouth with hers once again. She could remember no other time, no other circumstances.

A furious rattling sound brought them apart. 'I think I'd better get that syringe out before it explodes.' Nina was breathless.

'We'll have Cindy down here, wondering what's holding us up.' Mark watched, breathing hard, as Nina removed the injection equipment to a sterile cloth on the tray. 'She's so anxious to show me that she's made a start.'

'Toward looking after herself? Yes.' Nina smiled. 'I hope I've left her with something, Mark. Dave made her *want* to stop being helpless. I'd like to think I started teaching her how.'

'You have. And that's why I still don't want you to leave. Nina, just for a little while? Until she's found the strength to—' He waved his hand, indicating the house, but probably referring to Faye Calvert's neurotic hold over her daughter. '. . . to break out of the trap.'

'We'll talk about it later,' was all Nina promised. She had completed setting up the tray and now she picked it up. 'Will you follow me upstairs?'

'I'd follow you anywhere,' Mark said.

They exchanged the kind of secret smile lovers pass between them, the smile that says, 'We know something wonderful that no one else knows.'

Cindy might have guessed, had she not been excited about demonstrating her ability to inject air into insulin bottles. Nina would share her joy with Cindy later, when she had decided what to do about staying on the case, or when Mrs. Calvert had decided what to do about *her.* And Cindy's happiness for her new friend

125

would be genuine, Nina was certain. For now, while Mark was in the room, the girl was pleased enough with her progress toward independence. And if there was going to be any talk about newfound love, she was going to do the talking.

'That's forty-seven,' Mark said as he started to leave.

Nina frowned her incomprehension. Then, as he winked at her, she understood and laughed.

Cindy frowned. 'I don't get it. Forty-seven what?'

'Forty-seven times in twelve minutes you've mentioned Dave Tolson.'

Cindy blushed a becoming pink, then joined the laughter.

They were still laughing when Faye Calvert came to the doorway, dressed to the nines, to inform her daughter that she was going out. She left behind her the scowling impression that she knew no one particularly *cared* where she was going—that she would not be missed by anyone present, including her daughter.

Knowing Faye Calvert, Nina had a faintly disturbing thought; the woman would do something about that. But with Mark backing her up, Mark in love with her, Nina shrugged off the impression.

As soon as Mrs. Calvert's car was seen, from the bedroom window, backing out of the long driveway, Cindy resumed her wide grin and said, 'What's your rush, Mark? Sit down a minute. Or let's go downstairs. Want to go for forty-eight?'

'Can't,' Mark said. 'I've got a hospitalized patient to see. Two, actually. I'll see you both tomorrow.' He planted a brotherly kiss on Cindy's brow and said, 'I'm proud of you, neighbor.' He returned Cindy's glowing smile, hesitated, as though weighing the propriety of bussing a private-duty nurse while in the patient's room, then bent to place a long, lingering kiss on her lips. 'Call you tomorrow,' Mark said. He waved and he was gone.

Cindy was silent until the heavy, muffled sound of footsteps receded down the carpeted stairway. Then, in a sudden burst of excitement, she shouted, 'Oh, wow! Oh, *wow,* Nina! I was wrong, I was wrong, I was wrong!'

Before her lanky, long-haired patient had leaped across the room to smother her in a joyful embrace, Nina had time to murmur an ecstatic agreement. 'Uh-huh, Cindy. We were both wrong.'

CHAPTER NINE

By the end of the week, Mark's persuasive arguments had convinced Nina that it would only be a matter of time before Cindy would be able to regulate her own insulin therapy.

It was something the girl wanted to do, something she now associated with freedom from domination, with becoming a woman instead of remaining a helpless child, with Dave Tolson. Being able to *be* with Dave, married to Dave, living the rest of her life with Dave!

'I couldn't imagine Cindy becoming such an avid pupil,' Nina admitted. 'She's quit reading poetry. This afternoon she was studying *Diabetes As a Way of Life* by a Doctor Dankowski. Yesterday I drove her to the library and she came home with *A Primer for Diabetics*. I'm teaching her to give injections.'

'With an orange, I hope.'

'Grapefruit.'

Mark smiled, his fingers tightening over Nina's.

They were having dinner in a quaint Belgian restaurant in the business district of the North Shore suburb. Mrs. Calvert and the two women servants were at home with Nina's patient. Somewhat reluctantly, Cindy's mother had accepted the fact that Nina was entitled to evenings off, days off, weekends off, though the matter had never been discussed. She had resigned herself to sacrificing an evening with Ronald Perry, making the most of her martyrdom by saying she would *love* an evening with her daughter. She had narrowed her cold hazel eyes, however, when Nina's date for the evening came to call for her, and Mark

128

had gotten a distinctly chilly welcome into the house.

'It wouldn't be worth upsetting Cindy, for the short time you'll have to stay,' Mark said. Holding hands across the table still seemed like something out of a dream to Nina, yet the warm pressure of his fingers was excitingly real. 'You've got her on the right track, honey. Give her another month or so and she won't have to go through the business of adjusting to a new nurse. Because you've been so much more to her than that.'

Nina drank in the compliment as she drank in the admiration in Mark's eyes. 'It's getting rough.'

Mark nodded. Salads arrived. Their hands separated until the waitress disappeared into the shadows near the kitchen door, then they found each other again, the salads ignored. 'Faye wants you out. I know that. Believe me, you have my sympathy.'

'She's taken to standing over my shoulder, being picky and petty, questioning every move I make. And being careful not to do her criticizing while Cindy's around.'

'Did Dave call today?'

'He doesn't have to. He has a number at the dorm where he can be called now.'

Mark's features brightened. 'She calls him?'

Nina couldn't resist a proud grin. 'From the library, if her mother's home.' More seriously, she added, 'But she doesn't like having to do that, Mark. She's full of guilt about having to sneak behind her mother's back. And she's still convinced Mrs. Calvert's made tremendous sacrifices for her.'

'Making one tonight,' Mark observed. Reluctantly, their hands separated and they tackled spinach salads. 'Faye won't think so, once her lover-boy's taken her for a bundle and found himself an easier touch. A younger one, probably. You know, the average observer would wonder what Perry sees in her—a woman that much older, not an especially appealing personality. Of course, anyone with an ounce of sense knows. Money. It's as crass and as simple as that. But I keep wondering what Faye sees in that *creep.*'

Nina thought about it for a moment. 'Well, he's very attractive, in a foppish sort of way. He can be very charming. Actor type. He knows all the right words.'

'Other women falling all over him, I guess.' Mark shrugged. 'And he's all hers. I imagine that would be it. She's flattered. But she must know he's only using her.'

'Women in love never know that,' Nina said.

'*People* in love never know that,' Mark corrected. 'I know I didn't. It took me forever to make the discovery, and even then I was months admitting it to myself and making the break.'

Nina was wordless, not knowing what to say when Mark brought up the subject of his

130

unfortunate love affair. He had mentioned it several times in the past few days, as though he were running out an unpleasantness that he wasn't quite ready to forget.

'Well, you've given me the woman's angle on Perry. Attractive. Personable. Charming. I've only seen him as a Grade-A phony. So pompous that he makes me want to laugh. Male viewpoint.'

'*I* don't find him appealing,' Nina protested. 'In fact, he irritates me. I was furious with him one day when he started ridiculing the care we've tried to give Cindy. And then he started on that hocus-pocus about being able to "cure" her if we'd only apply his theories.'

Mark was looking at her with a sober, almost stern expression. 'What did he say, Nina?'

She tried to repeat Ronald Perry's words as well as she could remember them, but everything the man said was vague in her mind, perhaps because what he preached was vague. Then she remembered the telephone conversation she had overheard, at least Faye Calvert's part of it, and told Mark what she remembered. 'I had the feeling that she was being pressured, Mark.'

'Into applying what he preaches?'

'Yes. She talked about, oh, having faith in him. And she asked him to be patient. There was something about money, too, but I don't remember it too well.'

'*Her* money?'

'I got the impression that she was talking about Cindy's inheritance.' Nina hesitated. 'I could be wrong, Mark. It was just my impression. But she seemed to be worried about Cindy marrying Dave Tolson and needing that money. And she implied—I could be wrong again—she implied that if Cindy married someone else, the money wouldn't be important to her. It could go for whatever Mrs. Calvert and the "Reverend" wanted to use it.'

'If Cindy married someone else,' Mark repeated. 'She wasn't naming any names.'

'Did she have to?'

Mark made a shuddering motion. 'The woman's out of her mind.'

'You said that facetiously, Mark. I wish you'd heard her trying to convince Perry that she *does* believe Cindy'd be cured with his help—if you were out of the picture.'

Mark gave her a grave look. 'Keep your eyes and ears open, Nina. It's something I've been worried about ever since that character came along.'

Nina felt a brief queasiness, remembering what Dave Tolson had told her about why she had been hired. But the disquieting notion disappeared as Mark changed the subject, talking about their future together, hinting at marriage . . . without actually specifying that he wanted Nina to be his wife, talking about

132

the possibility of seeing Europe together in the coming year, when he'd fulfilled a number of time-consuming obligations that he'd taken on. Presidency of a regional medical society, for one thing. 'I'll be going to New York for the convention in a few weeks,' he said. 'After that, when we've got Cindy taking care of herself the way most diabetics do, you'll be free, dear. Then we can talk about how we're going to spend the rest of our lives.' Mark's eyes probed deeply into Nina's. 'Together?'

She looked down at the tablecloth, too overwhelmed by the gaze and by the promise. 'I hope so. Yes. It would be good, Mark. At least for me.'

'For both of us,' he said fervently.

They finished their dinner. Afterward, they took in a European comedy at a new little art-film theater nearby. When Mark saw her to the Calverts' door it was a quarter past eleven.

There were no signs of activity in the house. Mrs. Calvert had evidently gone to bed. Nina assumed that Cindy was asleep, too, but as she passed her door she noticed that a light streak shone from under the closed door.

Opening Cindy's door cautiously, Nina saw that the girl had fallen asleep with her bedside lamp still burning. Tiptoeing across the room, Nina checked the sleeping figure. Dark hair spread over the pillow, a soft half-smiling expression on her thin, delicate face, Cindy was sound asleep, almost angelic in her repose.

Nina reached out to click the lamp switch, then stopped her hand. On the bedside table were a stack of printed brochures she had never seen before. On top of the pile was a small booklet titled *The Medical Conspiracy.* A subtitle, in italicized letters, read, *The Hoax of Illness and Your Key to Perfect Health.* The author was Ronald Perry, his name followed by a series of initialed titles that Nina did not recognize.

Careful not to rustle the papers and waken Cindy, Nina glanced at the other titles. They were all along the same lines, implying that illness was a state of mind promoted by unenlightened or unscrupulous medical practitioners with a vested interest in keeping the truth from their ailing patients. There were at least fifteen booklets and tracts, all of them published by Ronald Perry's Temple of Universal Wisdom.

Nina set them back on the bedside table, turned off the light, and crept out of the room.

Faye Calvert, stuck at home, had not wasted the evening. Instead of poetry or information on diabetic control, Cindy had probably read herself to sleep with the reassuring, promising, esoteric vagaries on which her love-smitten mother had been gorging herself. The only difference was that Faye Calvert's faith in a phony cult leader might mean the loss of thousands of dollars which she could afford, whereas if Cindy were convinced that doctors were conspirators and insulin was an unnatural poison, her loss would be one that she could *not* afford.

But there was no need to be worried, Nina assured herself. There was Cindy's love for the young medical student. There was Cindy's profound respect for Mark Danover, her trust and affection for a nurse who was helping her toward physical independence. Mrs. Calvert's attempt to propagandize would have no effect as long as Cindy knew there were other people who cared about her. Medical people—Mark, Dave, Nina.

But what would happen if the nurse Cindy respected quit her job because she couldn't take Mrs. Calvert's harassment? If there was no one to encourage her romance with Dave Tolson, to see that the two young people were not cut off from each other as they had been before Nina intervened, what then? Cindy was far from being free of her mother's influence. Mark was too busy to supervise the girl's care on a day-to-day, hour-to-hour basis. If I leave, Nina thought, I may not be able to live with my conscience.

Mrs. Calvert's petty bickering became insignificant. As long as Cindy needs me, Nina promised, I'll be here.

CHAPTER TEN

Nina, in her determination to stay with Cindy, did not take into consideration Mrs. Calvert's equal determination to rid herself of a 'meddling employee.' Nor was it possible to foresee a totally unexpected circumstance.

Several days after Cindy had been deluged with material intended to turn her against the doctor and nurse who cared for her, the author of those pamphlets came to call. It was late afternoon, and Ronald Perry was admitted by the housekeeper. With Cindy in her room studying diet substitutions and menus for diabetic patients, and Faye Calvert in her suite, presumably getting ready for the arrival of her swain, Nina found herself alone with the latter in the drawing room, where she had been recording adjusted insulin requirements on Cindy's chart.

Constance Bell gave Nina a leering glance as she left the room. Ronald Perry's expression was no less impersonal.

'Writing your memoirs?' he asked.

'No, a suicide note,' Nina told him. Somehow, she couldn't help being snide around the man. His very presence was irritating.

'I suppose we all have those days,' he said, standing behind the secretary desk.

Nina kept her back to him, trying hard to concentrate on what she was doing. After a few seconds, when Ronald Perry gave no indication that he was going to stop looking over her shoulder, Nina attached her ball-point pen to the clipboard and decided to finish the job in her room. Leah was upstairs, making beds, and she had chosen this spot for privacy, but the maid would have disturbed her less than the visitor.

'We all have those days,' the self-proclaimed minister repeated. 'Especially in an atmosphere where there's so much conflict.'

Nina decided not to comment. She picked up the chart and got to her feet.

'I've been hoping your differences with Faye could be resolved. She's been unusually edgy the past few weeks. I sent some of our literature in hopes that you'd see why we think your efforts are being wasted.'

Nina shot him a disparaging look. She made up her mind not to let herself be baited.

'Did you have a chance to read any of it?'

'Do you mean the pamphlets Cindy's mother gave her? I glanced at them, yes.'

He was standing in her way again, green-blue eyes practicing their sexy stare. 'If you read with an open mind, you should at least be curious, if not impressed.'

'I *was* impressed,' Nina told him.

His eyes swept over Nina, indicating that he liked what he saw. 'Oh? I'd be interested in your comments.'

'I was impressed with the fact that what you're preaching is terribly dangerous. If a patient took you seriously, the results could be fatal.'

'You *do* have a closed mind. You fail to understand that I don't advocate giving up the medical crutches and expecting instant results. I'm not one of those on-the-spot faith healers who depend on mood hysteria for short-term effects. The cosmic wisdom requires study. Preparation. When enlightenment comes, however, the student knows *positively* that he or she has the power to cure himself or . . . herself.'

'But, from what I read, one of the first steps is to realize that medical care is nothing more than window-dressing.'

'I can prove that to you,' Nina was told.

'Mr. Perry, I don't want to get into a religious argument.'

'But this knowledge has nothing to do with religion. It's basic truth that dates back to time immemorial. Ancient wisdom that was forgotten in the plunge toward materialism and, fortunately, was preserved for us by a few Masters—hidden wisdom, but available again to those who have eyes to see, ears to hear.'

He sounded as though he had mounted a pulpit. Nina could imagine the deep, dramatically modulated voice addressing 'true believers' like Faye Calvert. There was

138

something hypnotic about the man's voice, his appearance, his self-assured approach to the subject. She felt nervous, suddenly, eager to separate herself from him. 'Please excuse me. I have work to do.'

He didn't move. 'You always seem to, when I'm around. Just because we can't agree, just because you've been so thoroughly conditioned, doesn't mean we can't be friends.'

'If you don't mind, I'd really . . .'

'I find you enormously challenging, dear. Enormously attractive.'

Nina didn't move aside fast enough. Ronald Perry's arms reached out in a swift motion, encircling her and pulling her close. In the next instant her mouth was being crushed under an expertly possessive kiss. When she recovered from the shock, struggling to free herself, Nina found herself helplessly immobile, held in a vicelike grip.

She might have been held in the unwelcome embrace longer, except for a shocked, throat-clearing sound from the doorway. Ronald Perry almost pushed her out of his arms, turning away to pretend deep interest in an abstract painting on the wall, demonstrating his talents as an actor by feigning complete nonchalance. He didn't see Faye Calvert standing in the open doorway, nor did the latter let him know that she was there. Hazel eyes glared hatred into Nina's for a split second, and then Cindy's mother disappeared.

139

Shaken, Nina stooped to pick up the clipboard which had fallen to the floor. Burning with anger, she wanted only to hurry out of the room. It would be impossible to explain what had happened to Mrs. Calvert. She was too enraged to tell Ronald Perry what she thought of him.

After a few seconds, he looked over his shoulder, determined that they were alone, and said, 'I thought, for a second, we had an audience.' His laugh was humorless, almost derisive. 'I tend to be melodramatic. My theatrical background.' He turned his sultry smile on Nina. 'You're not annoyed, are you? You must have enjoyed that as much as I did. Be honest with yourself, dear. I found it exciting.'

Nina pushed past him. 'I haven't been so thrilled since my dentist told me I'd have to have root canal work.'

She heard his disbelieving laughter as she stamped out of the room. When she reached her own quarters, shutting the door firmly behind her, Nina burst into tears. Angry, frustrated tears that didn't stop until it was time to start thinking of Cindy's gram-weighing pre-dinner lesson in the kitchen.

That lesson didn't take place. Less than an hour later, Nina was summoned to the living room by Mrs. Bell. 'Mrs. Calvert wants to talk to you,' the dour housekeeper said. She appeared secretive and enormously pleased, her expression telling Nina that she knew exactly what had happened and what the results would be.

Cindy was typing something—probably a letter, a poem, or a diet list—when Nina passed her room on her way to the stairs. The girl's door was closed. Nina walked downstairs to find Mrs. Calvert seated in an armchair, looking for all the world like the head of a medieval inquisition, dressed in a black caftan that emphasized her judgelike demeanor. Less comforting was Mark's presence. He had been summoned to this meeting, Nina was certain. He had not planned to be here this evening.

There was a brief, formal exchange of greetings between Nina and the doctor. Mrs. Calvert waited until they had said hello to each other, then waved her hand. 'Sit down, Miss Bateman. This will not take long.'

Mark was looking at her with a hurt, puzzled expression.

'I don't think I have to tell you why you're here,' Mrs. Calvert went on. 'I've already told Dr. Danover what I saw earlier. I don't think we have to go into detail. He agrees with me that, under the circumstances, I've been entirely too patient.'

Nina looked at Mark. He evaded her eyes. 'I don't care what you think,' she said. 'I happen to find Mr. Perry despicable. I didn't . . .'

'Please spare us and yourself the embarrassment of an explanation,' Mrs.

Calvert said. The venom in her voice chilled Nina. 'We've reached the point, Miss Bateman, where your presence is intolerable.'

Nina turned away from the hate-filled face. 'Mark . . . Doctor . . . I don't know what you've been told, but . . .'

'He's been told exactly what I saw! I don't think you're naïve enough to think anyone's going to believe that you didn't throw yourself at Reverend Perry. You'll do everyone a favor, including yourself, by packing your belongings and leaving this house as quickly as possible.' Mrs. Calvert glanced toward the stairway. 'Before my daughter's subjected to another of the emotional scenes you've created in this home.'

'Mark—' Nina's plea stopped short. Mark was staring at his hands, uncomfortable, caught in an embarrassing scenario that he wanted to escape. 'He forced himself on me! I was working on Cindy's chart when he came into the room and . . .' Nina's explanation sounded hollow. Mark was still avoiding her eyes, apparently believing what he had been told. (Believing what he *chose* to believe?) She felt a sickening churning in her stomach. How had she described Ronald Perry to him? *Attractive. Charming. A man who knew all the right words.* She had also told Mark that she loathed the man, but he was remembering only what he wanted to remember. Dumbfounded, Nina got up from her chair and stammered,

'You can't possibly think . . .' Mark was still looking at his hands, grossly uncomfortable. 'I know I don't want to go through this sort of petty bickering,' he said tersely. 'I have important work to do. If I've made a mistake, I apologize. I think it's best if we terminate the arrangement.'

Mrs. Calvert nodded, her eyes reflecting a vindictive triumph. 'I wanted Miss Bateman to hear you say that.' She rose to her feet grandly. 'I think the decent thing to do is to tell Cindy that you've been called away for . . . personal reasons, Miss Bateman. Some sort of, oh, family emergency. I'm sure you don't want to upset her.'

Nina felt drained of words. What Mrs. Calvert thought didn't matter. But Mark! He had been convinced that she was encouraging the advances of that cheap . . .

'I'm sorry, but I have to go,' Mark was saying. In a matter of seconds he was walking toward the door. 'I was on my way to the hospital when you phoned me, Faye.' He hesitated, then made his brusque way out of the room. 'I'm sure we can end the matter without . . .' His voice trailed off. Without looking at Nina, without giving her a chance to explain, he was gone.

'What did you tell him?' Nina cried. 'What makes you think I'd . . .'

'I don't think there's anything further to discuss,' Mrs. Calvert said icily. *'Tonight,* Miss

Bateman. As quickly as possible. I'll see that your check is mailed to you. And I'd appreciate it if you didn't disturb my daughter.'

Nina stared at her for a few seconds, then raced out of the room. *Mark had believed her!* He had talked about love and devotion and trust, but he had believed that she was capable of carrying on a sleazy intrigue with Ronald Perry! By morning, a new nurse would be here to take her place. Nothing mattered any more except getting out, running, forgetting that for a little while she had thought Mark trusted her, believed in her, loved her.

Too hurt for tears, Nina organized her personal belongings, cramming them into suitcases, slamming the lids shut. Cindy's typewriter was still clicking away when she passed her door. Nina paused for a moment, reluctant to leave without saying goodbye. Then, leaving her luggage on the stairway landing, she went back to her room, scribbled a brief note saying that her mother had suffered a sudden illness and that she would be in touch. The note was left on Nina's dresser. She carried her suitcases to the car, making three trips. If Mrs. Calvert or the two women who made up her household staff were around, they were discreetly inconspicuous. Nina loaded her luggage into the trunk and the back seat of her car.

Passing Mark's house, she began to cry. She

144

was still crying when she pulled up in front of the apartment she had shared with her mother and would now share again.

CHAPTER ELEVEN

Nina's return to the neat but shabby apartment was greeted with the same bland indifference that had been accorded her departure. Her mother inquired about her health, noted that Nina looked 'kind of puffy around the eyes,' and after being assured that her daughter was not hungry, Mrs. Bateman returned to the television movie from which she had torn herself away.

Nina did exactly what she had known she would do; she cried herself to sleep. Early the next morning, feeling somewhat presumptuous in wearing her white uniform, she walked to the Community Day Clinic and, to her relief, was welcomed with open arms. A short time later, processing the flow of humanity that needed free care, she was functioning as a nurse again. Tired, bewildered, hurt, she was nevertheless serving her intended purpose once more, almost relieved at being separated from Mark Danover. *Almost.* The pain of his mistrust, the realization that she might never see him again, was like a leaden weight in her heart. But here there was no need to apologize, explain, watch her words, or worry about whether someone would disapprove of what she was doing. Injections, sutures, weighing-in of mothers-to-be, words of advice and encouragement to people with chronic ailments, cheerful smiles to bolster patients who were showing improvement; this was what she had studied for, this was what she had been meant to do.

Work kept her from falling apart during the day. Evenings were something else. Several times, made nervous by the tedium of television programs, or of doing crossword puzzles because there was nothing else to do in the cheerless apartment, Nina thought of phoning Cindy Calvert. Mark would see to it that she had the proper care. By now, a new nurse was in charge. And there was the distinct possibility that Mrs. Calvert or Leah or Mrs. Bell would answer the phone, curtly demanding to know why she was calling. Nina postponed the ordeal.

By the end of the week, Nina was desperate enough to think of calling Mark Danover. Desperate enough, but not courageous enough. He knew where to reach her if he wanted to do so. If he didn't know her home number, it was available from the personnel department at the clinic. She worked through a Tuesday and then a Thursday, days when Mark normally put in his time as a medical volunteer, washing and setting her hair the night before, careful to have her makeup on straight, to look fresh and attractive, convinced that he would look her up when he arrived at the clinic. But there was no sign of him.

On Thursday afternoon, Nina ventured to the examining room where she and Mark had worked before she took on the Calvert case. Although she herself had been transferred to another department of the clinic, Mark would be there, she was positive. Nina summoned the courage to ask one of the other nurses about him, feigning a casualness that she did not feel.

'Dr. Danover?' the nurse said slowly. 'I know he used to come in on Tuesdays and Thursdays. He hasn't lately. If you want to get in touch, they probably have his phone number in Personnel.'

'But he hasn't been here?' Nina found herself fighting against incipient tears.

'Not for a few weeks,' she was told. 'He only came here when he could spare the time, as I recall. Somebody told me he's involved now with some big medical society. Oh, sure! Dr. Beam said something about his being out of town at some kind of convention.'

Nina returned to her room, where a staggering caseload of patients waited for attention. She worked, now, with a taciturn young doctor who seemed to resent what he was doing, resent the patients who had gotten themselves into a depressing variety of medical predicaments, resent the people who were assisting him. Nina felt like an automaton working beside him. She tried not to think about Mark, to erase him from her consciousness. A man who told you that he loved you should also believe in you. The fact that he had made no attempt to communicate with her was proof that his declaration of love was not to be taken seriously. Nina applied dressings, noted the progress of patients on endless charts, and kept herself busy. Crying herself to sleep became a way of life, and as time elapsed her hope faded. It had been a too-good-to-be-true dream and now it was over.

She had been back at the clinic for almost two weeks when one of the other nurses told her someone wanted to see her—someone who was sitting outside in the crowded waiting room. It was noon, Nina's lunch hour, before she was able to get away to see who her visitor was. She assumed, by then, that whoever it was would be gone.

She was almost across the waiting room, on her way to the small mama-papa luncheonette across the street, when Nina saw Dave Tolson.

He leaped up from one of the wooden folding chairs and hurried toward Nina. Usually bright and smiling, the gangly, auburn-haired young man appeared anxious—perhaps even grim. 'Nina. I didn't think I'd ever get to see you!'

Nina apologized for the delay. 'I knew you

were here. Knew *somebody* was here to see me, but we were just snowed under. I promised Dr. Sayers I'd only take twenty minutes for lunch.' Nina surveyed Dave's face and frowned. 'Something wrong?'

Dave nodded. 'Can we go somewhere and talk?'

'Across the street,' Nina said. 'Have you had lunch?'

'I'm too jittery to eat. I'll have a malt, or something. You don't know how long I've been trying to track you down.'

On their way out of the gray, unattractive building, Nina asked, 'Didn't you ask Mark? He knows I used to work here. He drove me home once. He knows where I live.'

'If Doc was around, I wouldn't be here,' Dave said. 'I wouldn't be losing sleep, either.'

They were seated in a red plastic booth, their orders taken by the portly Greek owner, before Dave explained himself. 'I'm about to go out of my head. Mark's in New York. Mrs. Proctor told me she'll hear from him tonight, and then I'll know where he's staying. Big medical confab. Nina, I'm worried about Cindy. Worried—that's the understatement of the year. I'm scared to death.'

'Why? She's got to be under a nurse's care. I know Mark wouldn't leave unless . . .'

'They got a nurse to take your place. Mrs. Calvert got rid of her the third day. Mrs. Proctor said she saw another lady around after that. In a white uniform, so I guess it was an R.N. But since Dr. Danover left, she hasn't seen anybody who looks like a nurse.'

'And the doctor doesn't know this?'

'I told you, he's out of town!' Dave's voice rose, edgy, revealing nervousness and lack of sleep.

'The thing that scares me is, they won't let me talk to her, Nina. I've called and called and I always get the same answer. Cindy's asleep. She's not feeling up to talking to anyone. I leave messages, but I don't get called back. Last night, I drove over there. Mrs. Calvert came to the door and just about slammed it in my face. And, then, this morning, when I called, that skinny crone . . . what's her name . . .'

'Mrs. Bell?'

'Yeah. Mrs. Bell. She started telling me Cindy was in bed and that she was sick. I asked her what was wrong and then . . . it was like somebody grabbed the phone out of her hand and slammed it down. I kept trying to call back, but I got a busy signal. I guess they took the phone off the hook.' Dave's eyes pleaded with Nina. 'What do I do now? I can't break into the place, force my way in. But the woman said Cindy's "very sick." If there's no nurse around and if they haven't called in another doctor . . .'

'They must have,' Nina said. She sounded positive, yet inwardly she was unsure. 'There'd

150

have to be *somebody.*'

Dave hadn't touched the malt that had been placed before him. 'I don't know,' he said. His voice sounded ragged. 'The last time I talked with Cindy . . . it was the afternoon after you left and she snuck over to the Danover house . . . called me out of a class . . . she was all shook. She said you'd left her high and dry. She was crying, Nina. She said you hadn't even said good-bye and you probably didn't care what happened to her.'

Nina felt a surge of raw guilt. 'I was fired, Dave. I was told to get out of the house immediately. Never mind why. And I thought it would be easier on Cindy if I just . . . made up some excuse and got out. I assumed there'd be somebody to take my place. Mark knew I was leaving.'

'There was. There was, but I'll swear there's nobody there now. And that's not what's driving me crazy.' Dave pushed his earnest, freckled face forward, his anguish clearly apparent. 'That last time I talked to her, Cindy was talking about . . . something she never talked about before. About maybe being wrong, putting all her trust in people like Mark. And you.'

Nina recalled the stack of pamphlets at the girl's bedside and drew in a quick breath. 'What did she say?'

'She said that maybe her mother was right. Not about me. Not about the two of us, but

151

about her getting "cured." Nina, I'm not out of med school, but I know she's never going to get "cured." She's going to live with diabetes all her life. I tried telling her that, telling her it's something a lot of people adjust to and learn to live with. But she was crying so hard, I know she wasn't listening to me. She said something about nobody really caring for her except her mother, and how her mother was showing her how she could rise above being sick by thinking the right kind of thoughts. She'd read something her mother gave her, something that proved she didn't have to go through life getting stuck with needles every day...'

'Dave! My God, do you know what that could mean?'

'Why do you think I've been going out of my mind? *Sure* I know what that could mean. What I don't know is what I can do about it. I can't call the police. I can't go barging into the house. Cindy's a minor. Her mother's got complete charge. *And her mother's out of her mind!*'

Nina's hand went to her forehead. 'You can't prove that, either. Dave, we've got to reach the doctor.'

'Sure. Sure, we'll do that. But that's something else I haven't told you. Something else that Cindy said, the last time we talked.'

'Mark didn't walk out on the case. No matter how much hassle there was, he wouldn't . . .'

'He didn't walk out. Mrs. Calvert told him his services were no longer required.'

Nina tried to digest the shocking news. 'It wouldn't matter. He still wouldn't leave town if he wasn't sure Cindy was under medical care. I know Mark. He just wouldn't abandon a patient that way. Especially not somebody he's fond of.' Nina thought over what she had just said. 'No, he wouldn't leave *anybody* who's sick. Not even somebody he hated.'

'So there was a new nurse coming in. Maybe Mrs. Calvert told him she was calling another doctor. You're right. He would have had to believe that. I know he wouldn't leave Cindy unless he believed that. The question is, what do we do now?' Dave was close to tears. 'She could be dying, for all we know. I didn't know anybody else to go to. I knew you'd care. The way Cindy talked about you, I knew you'd care.'

Nina felt her eyes misting over. Something had to be done, but what? A dismissed R.N. could no more burst into the home of a private patient than could an unwanted medical student. Mark. Mark was their only hope. 'Mrs. Proctor doesn't know where the doctor's staying?'

'No. He called her and said he was going to move out of the hotel he was in. To a more convenient place, closer to where the convention's being held. She's going to hear

153

from him this evening, she said.' Dave slammed a fist into his open palm. 'Nina, the very last thing I heard from Cindy was that if a person applied mental power, if a person really believed that sickness was an illusion and doctors just preyed on its victims . . . medicines wouldn't be needed. Surgery wouldn't be needed. You know what she was telling me? Not in so many words, but do you know what she was saying? *That she didn't need insulin!* Her mother had stood by her when the medical people walked out, and she believed in her mother!'

Nina muttered a fearful prayer under her breath. 'Oh, God.'

'I thought maybe you'd know what to do. You were her nurse. Maybe you could go back there and find out . . .'

'I wouldn't get past the door,' Nina said. 'I'm a lot less welcome in that house than you are, Dave. And you couldn't get in.'

Her mind was swirling with an overheard telephone conversation. Mrs. Calvert asking her 'spiritual adviser' to be patient, implying to him that she would begin to practice what he preached as soon as she had resolved a few personal problems. One of the obstacles had certainly been her inability to get Cindy and Mark together. If she had dismissed Mark, dispensed with his services, it was a sure sign that she had given up. She was free now to convince Ronald Perry that she was a true

154

disciple. And being a faithful follower meant
. . .

'Dave, we've got to reach Mark. As soon as possible.'

He nodded miserably. 'I don't know that he can do anything to help. But I can't think of anything else to do, either.'

Nina recalled her own days as a student. 'Do you have money? For calls?'

Dave's reddened face gave her the answer. 'Here.' Nina fished inside her purse, extracting several bills. 'Use this. Keep trying to call Cindy. As soon as you find out from Mrs. Proctor where Mark's staying, get on the phone and don't stop calling until you reach him.' She slipped the money to Dave as discreetly as possible and he pocketed it. 'And stay in touch with me.' She jotted down her home telephone number on a scrap of note paper and handed it across the table. 'I can't leave work. I would if I could, but it's just impossible today.'

'What time will you be home?' Dave asked. He seemed disheartened, as though he had looked for Nina a long time, and having found her, expected her to work an instantaneous miracle. 'I'll call you there, even if I haven't learned anything.'

'I get off duty at three. It takes me about ten minutes to walk home.'

Nina ate her lunch alone and in silence. Dave Tolson had headed for the nearest telephone booth, after getting change from the cashier. He was still in the booth when Nina decided that she couldn't finish her lunch, and left the small restaurant.

At quarter after three, Nina made her first attempt to call the Calvert home. Mrs. Bell answered after the third ring, said crisply that Miss Cindy was not able to come to the phone, and cut off the call before Nina was able to ask if her ex-patient was well. Dialing the number again, Nina wondered if she shouldn't have waited. Maybe Dave was trying to reach her. Possibly he had reached Mark.

This time, Nina's call resulted in a busy signal. After repeated attempts to call, followed by the insistent buzzing sound, Nina concluded that someone at the Calvert house had taken a phone off the hook. She paced the small apartment, trying to divert her thoughts by starting dinner. Her mother would get home from work at five-thirty and would welcome a hot meal.

It was impossible to think about anything except Dave Tolson's agonized face. And Cindy. Cindy listening to her mother— a lovesick, flipped-out fanatic—feeling abandoned by the people who wanted to help her, feeling deserted. And willing to try whatever Mrs. Calvert told her to try.

Nina gave up the thought of preparing dinner; something could be rustled up when her mother arrived. She waited a reasonable interval for a call from Dave, then tried the Calverts' number once again. This time, Faye Calvert's voice responded.

She sounded disappointed when Nina told her who was calling. 'Oh? I imagine you're calling about your check. I know it was mailed on . . .'

'I've gotten it, thank you.' For some reason, talking with Mrs. Calvert always made her shaky. Nina steeled herself to ask the question: 'I was wondering how Cindy's getting along.'

There was a short silence, as if Mrs. Calvert was deciding how to respond. Then she said, 'She's fine. Just fine. It's going to take some time for her to make the adjustment, but now that we've risen above all the . . . poison-pushing quacks, I'm sure she's going to do very well.' With exaggerated politeness, she added, 'Thank you for your concern. Will that be all?'

'Mrs. Calvert? By "poison," do you mean insulin?'

Another momentary pause. Then, proving to Nina that all was not as 'fine' as she was being led to believe, Mrs. Calvert said in a shrill, defensive tone, 'I know exactly what I'm doing, Miss Bateman. Cindy's my daughter, isn't she? Would I want anything but the best for my own child?'

'I'm sure you wouldn't, but . . .'

'A metaphysical cure doesn't happen overnight, you know. The patient has to understand how mind works over matter. It requires training. Education. *Faith,* Miss Bateman. You may be disappointed to know that Reverend Perry and I are working closely together. *Very* closely. And I have absolute confidence that Cindy will come out of . . . that she'll overcome this . . . temporary setback.'

'What kind of setback, Mrs. Calvert?' Nina's heart had started a thumping tattoo. 'Mrs. Calvert? What do you mean by a temporary—'

She was talking to herself. There was a loud clicking sound and then the steady hum of an open line; Mrs. Calvert had disconnected the call.

Nina's attempts to call again were frustrated by the monotonous sound that comes when a telephone is left off the hook. Wondering what to do, almost convinced that Cindy was being deprived of the vital insulin injections, Nina was considering what steps a dismissed R.N. could take, when Dave Tolson called.

'I didn't reach Doc personally,' he said, 'but I found out where he's staying. He was out, so I left a message.'

'To call you?'

'No, to call you. My phone at the dorm's always busy. And I left word it was an emergency regarding Cindy Calvert. You should be hearing from him soon.'

Nina decided not to tell him about her conversation with Mrs. Calvert. Dave was frightened enough without being told that Cindy would 'probably overcome this temporary setback.' Mark would call. He *had* to call. 'I forgot to ask where I can reach you,' Nina said. She wrote down the address and the telephone number Dave Tolson gave her. 'I'll be in touch,' she promised him.

'Tomorrow could be too late,' he said. 'I know . . . *you* know what can happen if she doesn't get . . .'

'We won't wait until tomorrow,' Nina promised. 'Tonight, one way or another . . .'

'We'll do something.' Dave sounded breathless, terrified. 'Nina, if I have to break the doors down I'll do it. I *love* her! If anything happens to Cindy, I don't know what I'd do. I really *love* her!'

Six o'clock passed and then seven. Nina prepared a hasty, indifferent dinner for her mother, who announced in a tired voice immediately afterward that she was going out to a bingo game. Nina cleared away the dishes, washed and wiped them, then put them away. At eight-thirty she was still sitting near the telephone, waiting for Mark's call, when the phone shrilled, stirring her out of her chair. Edgy, she said, 'Hello?'

The caller was not Mark Danover. A choked, barely coherent voice said, 'Miss Bateman? You've got to get here at once. There's something terribly wrong. I *know* it's going to be all right if I just keep holding up the highest thoughts for her, but right now—' Faye Calvert's voice dropped to a strange whisper. *'Right now, I think you should be here. As fast as possible.'*

Nina erased her past hostility toward the woman. Mrs. Calvert was terrified. 'What's wrong, Mrs. Calvert? Can you tell me what's wrong?'

'I can't think of anyone else to call,' Mrs. Calvert said. She sounded like someone calling from another planet, dazed and sing-songy, barely making sense. 'You were her nurse. It's your duty. Nurses have duties, don't they? Even though you've been paid off, don't you still have some kind of . . . moral duty?'

'I'll be there, Mrs. Calvert. Tell me what's wrong.'

'I thought . . . well, I've been treating her . . . mentally, of course . . . treating her for the flu. Spring flu. Not that it's a real disease. There *are* no real diseases, you know. But Cindy isn't sufficiently advanced to know that.'

'Mrs. Calvert, please! Tell me . . .'

'She was terribly thirsty. Drank and drank and drank. We couldn't get enough water to her. But she couldn't keep it down. She couldn't keep *anything* down, food *or* water. And she complained of a pain. Abdominal pain.'

'Is her face flushed?' Nina asked quickly. 'Is she having trouble breathing?'

'Gasping. Yes.' Faye Calvert might have been talking from another world. She had lost her imperious tone, sounding as though she were trying to understand the impossible thing that was taking place. 'And then she fell into a sound sleep. She's sleeping so soundly, Miss Bateman, that I can't wake her up.'

'Have you called a doctor?'

There was no response.

'Mrs. Calvert, I think you'd better call an ambulance!'

There was a heavy breathing sound on the other end of the line, but no reply.

'Call Mercy Hospital. Unless you have a new doctor you can call?'

'No doctor,' Mrs. Calvert said adamantly. 'We've had all we want to do with doctors.'

Nina didn't question her as to why she had called upon a nurse. The woman was obviously deranged. But some shred of intelligence, or some instinct, had remained, telling her to seek help. 'Mercy Hospital. The Emergency Room,' Nina told her. 'Have them send out an ambulance as quickly as possible.'

'An ambulance?' The voice had taken on its old superior tone. 'I don't think we have to go that far. Ron's going to be here shortly. I called and he promised he'd come. I just wanted to make sure . . .'

'Mrs. Calvert, Cindy's probably gone into an acidosis coma. She needs medical attention and she needs it fast. Will you do as I say? Call the hospital?'

'Well . . . if you say so. Though it seems like a terrible breach of . . . faith.'

161

Before Nina could explain to her why the call was vitally important, Mrs. Calvert had sighed, repeating, 'Well, if you say so.'

'I'll be there as soon as I can,' Nina told her. 'I hope, when I get there, that Cindy will be at the hospital.'

There was an incoherent muttering on the other end of the line and then Nina heard the now-familiar clicking sound again.

She raced to get her handbag, started out the door, and then paused before the telephone. Quickly, she dialed the number that Dave Tolson had given her. It seemed as though hours had gone by before she reached him.

'Dave, I got a call from Mrs. Calvert. Cindy's in a coma, I think. From the symptoms she described, it sounds like an acidosis coma.'

'My God!' Dave rasped the words. 'Have you heard from Doc?'

'Not yet. I'm going over there, Dave. She must . . . Mrs. Calvert must have been very frightened if she lowered herself to call me. I can stop by for you.'

'Please. Yeah, please do that.'

They arranged a meeting place—a corner near Dave's dormitory that would take Nina out of her way but wouldn't involve wasted time looking for his address.

Nina was locking up the apartment when the telephone started ringing. It might be Mark, or it might be someone who didn't matter—one of her mother's card-playing cronies. Nina started to unlock the door again when the phone stopped ringing. She hurried to the parking area behind the old apartment house. By the time she picked up Dave Tolson, she was repeating the same prayer over and over to herself. They drove toward the North Shore suburban home of the Calverts without exchanging more than a few words. Dave was praying, too. Even a first-year medical student knew what an acidosis coma, allowed to go untended, could mean to a diabetic patient.

CHAPTER TWELVE

Ronald Perry's sports car was parked in the Calvert driveway; Nina braked her car next to it, then she and Dave ran to the front door.

'I hope she's not here,' Nina said. 'I hope they've gotten Cindy to a hospital.'

Dave was too terrified for words. He made a nodding assent and kept running. Someone must have been watching for Nina's car; the door was flung open before they reached it. Mrs. Bell, more dour than usual, stepped aside.

'Where's Cindy?' Nina demanded.

Mrs. Bell indicated the stairway with a gloomy look. 'Up there. She's not in no shape to be goin' anywhere.'

Nina glared at her. 'Get an ambulance here! And call Emergency at Mercy Hospital!'

'I don't trust her,' Dave said. 'I'll do it, Nina.' He was racing for the nearest telephone as Nina pounded up the stairs.

Faye Calvert and Ronald Perry were in the hallway outside Cindy's room. Nina heard their loud argument before she was halfway up the stairs.

'I never told you to take her off insulin!' Ronald was insisting. 'She wasn't anywhere ready. Neither are you!'

'Ron, honey, you said I was the most spiritually advanced . . .'

'Will you stop being ridiculous? I don't know why you got me over here. Get the kid to a doctor. I can't do anything for her!'

'Ron, you can! You know you can! They'll just pump more poison into her at a hospital. You know the secrets of the hidden wisdom. You could go in there and . . .'

'Will you shut up? Sick people bug me. Get somebody over here and stop trying to involve me!'

'You kept telling me she didn't need medical care! Ron, you were angry with me because . . .'

'Not as mad as I am right now. Let me get out of here . . . I've got a class waiting for me.'

'If you leave me now, I'll . . . there won't be any more checks, Ron. I'm warning you, not one more thin dime.'

'I'm doing fine without your damned checks, you hysterical old bag!'

Nina brushed past them, her arrival barely acknowledged except for Mrs. Calvert's, 'Maybe *she'll* know what to do.'

Cindy's door was partially open. Nina pushed her way into the room, dreading what she might see as she approached Cindy's bed. She was both alarmed and relieved by the sound of a gasping breath. Cindy was unconscious, her face drained of color, but she was alive. The labored breathing, indicative of air hunger, verified Nina's worst fears; Cindy was suffering an acidosis coma. Leaning close, Nina caught the sweetish odor of the girl's breath. Ketone bodies had caused an acidosis, throwing off the hydrogen-ion balance in Cindy's body. The body was trying to compensate by releasing carbonic acid through Cindy's lungs; her breath was deep, abnormally rapid, labored.

'Bring me the insulin and a syringe,' Nina ordered.

Mrs. Calvert was standing in the doorway, Ronald Perry sulking behind her.

'There isn't any insulin,' Mrs. Calvert said.

'There's got to be! There was a supply in the refrigerator. I'm sure if there was another nurse here . . .'

'She didn't need it,' Mrs. Calvert said. She sounded either drunk or dazed, like someone speaking from out of a trance. 'I threw out all those horrible needles. There's . . .'

Nina cursed her, and the woman drew in a shocked breath. 'Dave?' She ran out into the hall. 'Dave, have you reached the hospital?' Calling down the stairs brought no response. Apparently Dave was still on the telephone.

Mrs. Calvert had recovered from hearing what Nina thought of her. 'Is there something you can do? I haven't been able to wake her up. And she kept vomiting . . .'

'Look, I'm not serving any purpose here,' Ronald Perry grumbled.

They resumed their argument, Mrs. Calvert pleading with him to stay, to apply his esoteric 'powers,' to *do* something, anything.

Nina returned to the bedside, her mind racing with instructions she had memorized during her training and in talking with Mark Danover. Cindy had to be rushed to a hospital. That was the first consideration. In the meantime, what? Take a blood sample. There was no way to make a test here. Cindy's body was dehydrated—a dangerous lack of water and minerals. The hospital again. And a massive amount of insulin was desperately needed, then blood or plasma. Nina could only imagine the level of blood sugar that was playing havoc with Cindy's imbalanced system.

She felt helpless. As helpless as an untrained layman. Nina touched Cindy's forehead with her fingertips. 'Hang on,' she whispered. 'You're going to be all right. Dave's here and I'm here, honey. Just . . . please hang on!'

In her own way, she was applying the mind-over-matter, will-to-live theories that Ronald Perry had preached and now abandoned. *Insulin*. Nina prayed silently, 'Please, God. Get the ambulance here. Insulin. She's got to have insulin!'

She heard someone pounding up the stairway and then Mrs. Calvert shrieking, 'What are you doing here? Who gave you permission to come into this house?'

Nina hurried toward the door.

'Ambulance on the way,' Dave panted. 'I couldn't reach a doctor, but the nurse in Emergency said there were two residents standing by. Nina, how is she? She's not . . .'

'She's in a coma, Dave. We didn't get here a second too soon.'

Dave was standing over Cindy's bed, tears forming in his eyes as he watched her struggle to fill her lungs with air. 'Did you give her an injection?'

'There's nothing to inject. Nothing to inject with.'

Their eyes met, Nina's telling Dave that breaking Mrs. Calvert and her 'adviser' in two wouldn't help the situation.

Dave pressed a thumb and forefinger into his eye sockets, shaking his head. 'What's keeping them?'

He had just called the ambulance, but an

eternity had already gone by. 'There's a car coming up the driveway,' Nina said. She had stationed herself at the window, watching. 'I think it's . . .'

'They said they'd hurry,' Dave said weakly. He had uncovered his eyes and was staring at Cindy again, one hand covering hers. Unconscious, she was still fighting to draw a life-giving breath.

'It's not an ambulance.' Nina peered out into the darkness below. 'Dave, it's just a . . . it's a taxi, I think. Yes. It's a cab.'

It wasn't 'just a taxi.' Seconds later someone else was hurrying up the stairs. Nina heard Mrs. Calvert shriek, 'You! Where've you been? Cindy's been *dying*, and you were off somewhere . . .'

'I was taken off the case!' It was Mark's voice, thick with rage. And then he was in the room, demanding to know if an ambulance had been called, if Cindy had been given . . .'

'Mrs. Calvert threw the insulin away,' Nina told him. She looked hopefully at the black bag he held in his hand.

Mark was unzipping it. 'I caught the first plane when I got your message. I assumed she'd be at the hospital, but I stopped at home to get my bag. There were lights on up here and I thought, 'My God, what if they didn't have sense enough . . . ?' Mark was removing a syringe from his armamentarium. Nina made a choking cry as he lifted out a familiar looking

168

bottle.

'Can I help?'

Nina's offer was waved aside. 'This isn't going to be a normal dose,' Mark said. 'There's alcohol in my bag. And cotton. Swab around a vein. I'm going to go into a vein . . . faster results.'

Nina sprang into action. Now, at least there was something to *do!*

Dave stepped away from the bed, getting out of the way. Outside the room, Faye Calvert and Ron Perry were still arguing—a loud, senseless argument full of accusations and denials. Then perhaps Ronald Perry reconsidered the possible loss of Mrs. Calvert's largesse. He was saying, 'Stop using up your mental power with petty matters, darling. Hold a high, positive thought. Cindy is incapable of illness. I do . . . I *do* hereby affirm that she is well. She is *well.*'

Entranced, Mrs. Calvert repeated, 'I affirm that we have the power and that *she is well.*'

Mark had pulled a large amount of fast-acting insulin into the barrel of the syringe. Nina found an easily available vein in Cindy's arm, swabbing the area around it with alcohol.

'You *did* call an ambulance?' Mark asked. He plunged the needle into Cindy's vein. She made a sharp moaning sound, then resumed her efforts to satisfy her hunger for air.

'I see headlights coming up the street.' Dave had taken over Nina's station at the window.

Mark didn't have to be told that they had done the right thing. He released the insulin into Cindy's vein, then withdrew the needle. 'I'll go in the ambulance with her,' he said. 'You two follow.'

'Doc?' Dave had turned away from the window. He was crying openly now, huge tears coursing down his freckled face. 'Cindy's going to be okay, isn't she? If I didn't think she was going to be all right, I . . . Doc, I wouldn't want to *live!*'

Mark was not untouched, but he kept the situation under control. Without giving Dave a guarantee that couldn't be given, he said, 'We're doing all we can. Thank God you called me . . . called that ambulance.'

Dave was looking down toward the driveway again. 'They're here.'

'Better run down and open the door for them,' Mark said. Dave was on his way when Mark said, 'She's *got* to make it, Nina.'

They faced each other for the first time since Mark had come into the room. 'It's bad, isn't it?'

Mark waited until the medical student was out of earshot. 'I'm not giving up, but I'm not too hopeful. What's the matter with these people?' The angry cry was followed by a subdued admission. 'I shouldn't have gone away. You shouldn't have left her, Nina. I know you were ordered out, but I shouldn't have let you go. Both of us know what an

170

emotional disturbance can do toward . . . plunging a patient into an acidosis coma. If she doesn't make it, I'll have her on my conscience for the rest of my life.'

There wasn't time to respond. Dave was leading two white-uniformed ambulance attendants up the stairs. They carried a rolling gurney between them, obviously aware of the urgency of their mission, wasting no time.

Nina was helping Mark and the attendants move Cindy to the palette when she heard Faye Calvert say, 'Oh, no, no! They aren't going to take Cindy out of this house!'

Ronald Perry muttered something unintelligible.

'We're working on her. We're succeeding, aren't we, Ron? She's going to rise above this illusory illness. I know she is! You've lifted her up out of it, Ron. You and I . . . we *know* she's going to be well, and her place is here with me!'

Insane words, pouring out of a deranged mind! As the attendants reached the hallway, Mrs. Calvert stretched out her arms to prevent their passage. They stopped, reluctant to move past her, looking to Mark Danover for instructions.

'You can't take her away,' Mrs. Calvert was saying. 'She's my child. She's a minor. You can't take her out of this house without my permission.'

'She's going to die if we don't get her out of

171

this house,' Mark warned her.

'Mrs. Calvert, please!' Dave's beseeching voice was lost in the rise of others. 'Please, for once in your life, don't hurt her. Please let the men go by!'

'Let them go,' Ronald Perry said. 'It can't do any harm.'

'You won't trust me again. You'll think I don't believe in you. *I affirm!*' Mrs. Calvert screeched. *'I affirm that I have the wisdom and the power—'*

Mark stepped in front to the ambulance attendants. 'Affirm it when and if we get her back to you,' he said. His hands closed over Mrs. Calvert's wrists, pulling her aside. She started to scream, and Ronald Perry protested, 'Now, look here, Danover, she has every right . . .'

'She doesn't have the right to murder a human being,' Mark spat out. He let go of Mrs. Calvert's wrists as she struggled to free herself, then gave her a shove that sent her against the corridor wall.

Mrs. Calvert was screaming like a banshee as the attendants filed past her and started down the stairs. 'She's not of age! I'll sue you! I'll sue you for every penny you've got! I'm the only one who can give permission, and I refuse to let Cindy fall into . . .'

'Nina? Do something.' Mark was tired. He was exhausted and worried. But he wasn't ready to give up. 'Cindy's birthday was two days ago. She's eighteen. She doesn't have to wait until she's twenty-one until she's free of you and financially independent.'

Ronald Perry drew in a sharp breath. 'Faye, you told me her money was tied up until . . .'

'Nina, please. Do what comes naturally!' Mark had cleared the way so that the stretcher could be maneuvered down the stairs.

As Mrs. Calvert made an insane leap to stop the man carrying the head of the stretcher, Nina grabbed her arm and spun her around. Fury gave her strength. Mrs. Calvert lunged toward her, hands upraised, fingernails poised to inflict cat-like damage. Cindy had to get to the hospital. And Mark had said, 'Do what comes naturally.' What came naturally was a swing of Nina's fist, her arm tracing a wide arc and landing on Mrs. Calvert's jaw.

The woman cried out one more time, her eyes bulging. Then, her body leaning against the wall, she slid down to the carpeted floor, silent and unseeing.

'Now, look here!' Ronald Perry hadn't wanted to become involved, but he registered his protest, nevertheless. 'You're supposed to be an angel of mercy, you little—'

Mark didn't let him finish the sentence. Perhaps it was his weariness, perhaps an accumulated hatred for the man who had disparaged his profession and made fun of his dedication. Or, perhaps it was only an urgency to get Cindy Calvert to a hospital. Finally, it may have been the ugly tirade the phony had been about to heap upon Nina's head. Mark wasn't a violent man, but this was a desperate, violent moment. His arm shot upward from out of nowhere. Nina heard the crack of knuckles against flesh. In another instant, Ronald Perry was stumbling backward in the hallway, losing his balance as he lost consciousness, and then collapsing to the floor like a limp puppet whose strings have been cut.

The ambulance men were down the stairs by then, Dave Tolson leading the way.

'Good show,' Mark said as he started down the stairs.

'Good show, yourself,' Nina responded.

Under other circumstances, they might have smiled at each other. Running, helping the attendants get Cindy into the ambulance, there was neither the time nor the inclination for smiles of satisfaction.

Following the ambulance, with Dave Tolson at her side, Nina forgot that Mrs. Calvert and Ronald Perry existed. She was praying again, her prayers more hopeful now that she knew Mark Danover was up ahead in the ambulance, doing whatever he could to keep Cindy Calvert alive.

CHAPTER THIRTEEN

Occasionally, as they paced the hospital corridor, Nina or Dave would make some inane, time-filling, emotion-concealing remark.

'I didn't know it was Cindy's birthday,' Dave said once. 'She didn't tell me. And I didn't even send a card.'

'I didn't know, either,' Nina told him. She checked her watch and then the clock on the wall above the nurses' station. 'I wish Mark would come out and tell us what's happening.'

After this, Nina knew, she would have a deeper understanding of the suspense and agony experienced by loved ones who walked a hospital corridor, waiting and wondering.

It was close to midnight before Mark joined them. He wasn't smiling, but, then, he wasn't looking dismal, either.

Dave rushed up to him. 'How is she?'

Mark patted him on the shoulder. 'We're over the hump, Dave. She'll be a day or more recovering. Maybe three or four more days convalescing. But she's going to be all right.'

The doctor and Nina pretended they didn't see a lanky, full-grown, auburn-haired adult dropping into one of the plastic settees in the waiting room, covering his face with his hands, and crying like a relieved child.

'Coffee time,' Mark said. 'Way overdue. Coffee time.' He released a tired sigh. 'I can't believe I was in New York at noon. I was supposed to be delivering a paper this evening.' He sighed again. Nina led him to a coffee machine at the end of the corridor.

When they had settled themselves in chrome and plastic chairs in a little waiting alcove, Nina said, 'What did you do?'

'Got a blood test. Poured more insulin into her. Blood transfusion. Potassium. Glucose, I.V.' Nina scowled. *'Sugar?'*

'That's a contradiction, I know.' Mark sipped at the steaming black coffee in his cup. 'Thing is, the blood sugar is dangerously high, but the actual amount of sugar in the patient's body fluids is way down. After we get the insulin working, the sugar level takes a nose dive. If the insulin's going to do its job, you have to start glucose to be on the safe side.'

Nina nodded, not quite comprehending. There was so much more she had to learn! She said it aloud. 'I've got so much more to learn.'

'I want Dave to learn it, too,' Mark said. 'And Cindy. Not just because I'm interested in the kid's medical education, but because he's going to be responsible for her. I want to pick up his education where you left off with Cindy's.'

Nina felt crushed with guilt. 'I didn't get very far, Mark. I wish I could have stayed. Prevented this awful . . .'

176

'I'm to blame for that,' Mark said. 'I should have flown into Faye's face and told her she *had* to keep you on. Why do you think I'm feeling so guilty?'

'Because you went away. And you weren't really sure Cindy was going to get the care she needs.'

'No.' Mark was shaking his head. 'No, that's not it. If I had insisted that you stay with Cindy, her mother would have given in. She's a weak-minded creature, easily influenced. And if I had put my foot down, made you realize how important you were to the kid, you'd have stayed. Hell, high water, or a card-carrying witch, you'd have stayed.'

Nina admitted that this was true.

'So why didn't I say anything? Because I was jealous. I was, face it, I was furious. Hurt and furious.'

'About *what?*'

'You letting that creep make a pass at you.'

'Mark, I didn't! I'll swear I didn't! You saw him tonight. He sways whichever way the wind blows. His principles are based on whatever occurs to him at the moment. Whatever he thinks is going to be good for him. He doesn't care a hoot about me or about Mrs. Calvert or about Cindy or about all the people who pay him good money because they think he's some kind of . . . some sort of all-knowing guru. I wanted to brain him, Mark! When he kissed, me, my stomach turned over and I wanted to do . . . I wanted to do what you did tonight. Knock him on his behind!'

Nina's impassioned argument ended on a silly note; she laughed at her own crudeness and suddenly Mark was laughing, too, in spite of his tiredness and the strain he'd been under. 'Apart from the fact that it was necessary,' he said when his laughter had died down, 'what I did tonight felt good.'

'Clobbering him the way you did? I'll bet it did.'

'And you, too. You must have wanted to clip Faye from the second I introduced you to her.'

'I wanted to throttle her.' Nina thought for a moment and then said, 'I'm not so sure I feel that good about it now, Mark. She's a sick woman. Every bit as sick as Cindy. Maybe more so. Maybe one of us . . . both of us . . . ought to stop over there and see how they're doing.'

'They've got the mysterious wisdom to get themselves together again,' Mark said. Sobering, he added, 'Okay, maybe we'll stop by. That's not where I'm going to end this, though. Perry's a menace. I don't have any doubt that Faye took her kid off insulin because she really believed that phony. He was denying his influence because he was afraid of what might happen, but he'll be back hustling money from credible fools like Faye as soon as he knows Cindy's all right. And I'm going to stop him, Nina. I don't know how. Not yet. But

I'm going to stop him before somebody else commits murder in the name of his blasphemous so-called "religion."'

'Call on me if you need a witness,' Nina said.

They talked for a long time after that, about what the future held for everyone concerned. 'Faye needs a shrink, there's no doubt in my mind about that,' Mark said. 'Maybe she'll see it now that lover-boy's let her know where he stands. She's got to know by now that he's no miracle-worker. That he wants out when the going gets rough. And when I slap him with a suit . . . or whatever it is that my attorney tells me I can do to put him out of business, Faye's going to see the light. The guy's bled her for money, made a fool of her, and nearly pushed her into a murder rap. She'll need help. Hopefully, she'll see that for herself. And it's a cinch she's not going to get custody of Cindy. If she does, it'll be over my dead body.'

'What about Cindy?' Nina asked.

'I haven't had time to think about it yet,' Mark admitted. 'But just off the top of my head, what if she came to stay at my place?'

'Her mother'd love that,' Nina said.

'Her mother isn't going to be around to like it or not like it. I told you, Faye's got her marbles mixed up. She'll be in even worse condition when she starts thinking about what Perry did to her. Anyway, Cindy's of age. She can make her own decisions. And the family attorney happens to be a good friend of mine. My own lawyer, as a matter of fact. So I don't think we'll have to worry about putting Cindy back in her mother's hands.'

'Dave?' Nina asked.

'Dave's still too young. He's not ready for a big responsibility. Sick wife, money worries.' Mark stared into the plastic cup for a few seconds. 'Maybe you can help me get this across to him, Nina. The whole ridiculous money thing. I have so much faith in his becoming a great doctor that I'd be willing to help him through school. If he won't accept help from me, maybe we can talk him into accepting it from Cindy. People who love each other shouldn't let their plans get messed up because of some silly pride. It would give Cindy a new impetus, I think. And it's obvious that sooner or later they're going to get married. If Faye couldn't stop it, there's nobody on God's green earth who can.'

Nina agreed with that statement, too. Then she said, 'I could teach Miss Proctor the things she has to know. She's very sharp and she's conscientious. Before we can teach Cindy to take care of herself, Mavis Proctor would be an ideal assistant.'

'After tonight, I'd still like to have an experienced R.N. around. At least until Cindy's ready to go out on her own.'

Nina was silent. Was he asking her to join the staff at his house? With Mark you never knew. He was tired; maybe he was just talking. And he had talked before, implied promises before.

'You, Nina,' he said suddenly. His hand had reached out for hers. 'I'd like *you* to be there when Cindy comes home. There's plenty of room. After a while, if you can see things my way, you wouldn't need a room of your own.'

Nina's breath quickened. Still nothing to say. She was afraid to ask Mark what he meant by the remark.

Astoundingly, as he tossed his paper cup into a nearby wastebasket, he was smiling. 'I'm a fairly decent medic, I think. But as a Romeo, I'm a dismal flop. Do you know what I'm trying to tell you, Nina? That I've behaved like a jealous, unreasonable high school freshman. I love you. I got it into my head that it was too good to be true . . . you actually being in love with me, too. I'd had that stupid experience. As though you and Jean had anything in common.'

Nina narrowed her eyes. 'Who's Jean?'

Mark had taken Nina's hands, pulling her up to her feet. 'I thought I'd told you. She made me think . . .'

'Made you think that she loved you. And wasn't ready to give up loving anybody else. Somebody as repulsive as Ron Perry?' Nina made a face indicating disgust. 'I've never met Jean, Mark. I never want to. *I could learn to hate her without even trying!*'

Mark stopped laughing as he pulled Nina into his arms. 'That's the most encouraging statement I've heard tonight,' he said. After he had kissed her once, and again, and then for the third time, he said, 'Oh, Nina . . . me thinking you didn't really love me, you going back to the clinic and thinking I didn't worship the ground you walk on! Maybe we can get a deal from Faye Calvert's shrink. Three for the price of one. We had to be out of our fool minds!'

He was kissing Nina again when Dave Tolson came up the corridor. 'I hate to break up a good thing,' he said, 'but I had to tell you. The nurse let me into Cindy's room. She opened her eyes. She had a sip of water. And now they want you, Doc. To tell them if it's okay to give her some tea with sugar, or some broth.'

Mark was the efficient M.D. again. 'I'll go check,' he said brusquely. As he started toward Cindy's room, he turned to tell Nina, 'Don't go away. Stay right where you are.'

Nina stayed exactly where she was. Dave stayed with her, alternately laughing and crying, telling Nina how much he owed to her, how thankful he was to Mark Danover, how much . . . how *terribly* much he loved Cindy Calvert.

He was good company, Nina thought. He distracted her mind from the long waiting period before Mark would return and they would go, together, to check on Mrs. Calvert and to tell her that her daughter was out of danger.

Ronald Perry would have regained consciousness by this time. Apart from a loose tooth or two, he would be none the worse for wear. But it would be good to make the call, anyway. Make the call and clear the decks for a totally new arrangement. Mavis Proctor, Cindy, Dave Tolson, Mark, and—

And *me*, Nina reminded herself. It was a comforting, exhilarating, wonderful thought that would make up for the discomfort of telling the nursing supervisor at Community Day Clinic that she was quitting her job again.

Dave was blotting his eyes with a ragged Kleenex, his back turned to Nina because he didn't want her to see him crying. 'It's going to be all right,' he sniffed. 'Everything. It's going to be okay.'

'Better than all right,' Nina told him. 'Better than okay.' She thought of how much Cindy loved him, of how determined Mark was that Dave would realize his ambition and emerge as a full-fledged M.D. Add Cindy to that picture. Add Mark to *mine*, Nina thought. 'It's going to be a whole lot better than all right and okay,' she said. And didn't wonder why Dave Tolson's head only nodded in reply, there being no words left to be said.